COLD CASE

COLD CASE

M A COMLEY

2017

New York Times and USA Today bestselling author M A Comley
Published by Jeamel Publishing limited
Copyright © 2017 M A Comley
Digital Edition, License Notes

All rights reserved. This book or any portion thereof may not be reproduced, stored in a retrieval system, transmitted in any form or by any means electronic or mechanical, including photo-copying, or used in any manner whatsoever without the express written permission of the author, except for the use of brief quotations in a book review or scholarly journal.

This is a work of fiction. Names, characters, places and incidents are a product of the author's imagination or are used fictitiously, and any resemblance to actual persons living or dead, business establishments, events or locales is entirely coincidental.

ISBN-13: 978-1545396704

ISBN-10: 1545396701

OTHER BOOKS BY M A COMLEY

Blind Justice (Novella)
Cruel Justice (Book #1)
Mortal Justice (Novella)
Impeding Justice (Book #2)
Final Justice (Book #3)
Foul Justice (Book #4)
Guaranteed Justice (Book #5)
Ultimate Justice (Book #6)
Virtual Justice (Book #7)
Hostile Justice (Book #8)
Tortured Justice (Book #9)
Rough Justice (Book #10)
Dubious Justice (Book #11)
Calculated Justice (Book #12)
Twisted Justice (Book #13)
Justice at Christmas (Short Story)
Prime Justice (Book #14)
Heroic Justice (Book #15)
Shameful Justice (Book #16)
Unfair Justice (a 10,000 word short story)
Irrational Justice (a 10,000 word short story)
Seeking Justice (a 15,000 word novella)
Clever Deception (co-written by Linda S Prather)
Tragic Deception (co-written by Linda S Prather)
Sinful Deception (co-written by Linda S Prather)
Forever Watching You (DI Miranda Carr thriller)
Wrong Place (DI Sally Parker thriller #1)
No Hiding Place (DI Sally Parker thriller #2)

Cold Case (DI Sally Parker #3)
Deadly Encounter (DI Sally Parker thriller series #4)
Web of Deceit (DI Sally Parker Novella with Tara Lyons)
The Missing Children (DI Kayli Bright #1)
Killer On The Run (DI Kayli Bright #2)
Hidden Agenda (DI Kayli Bright #3)
Murderous Betrayal (Kayli Bright #4 coming June 2018)
The Caller (co-written with Tara Lyons)
Evil In Disguise – a novel based on True events
Deadly Act (Hero series novella)
Torn Apart (Hero series #1)
End Result (Hero series #2)
In Plain Sight (Hero Series #3)
Double Jeopardy (Hero Series #4)
Sole Intention (Intention series #1)
Grave Intention (Intention series #2)
Devious Intention (Intention #3)
Merry Widow (A Lorne Simpkins short story)
It's A Dog's Life (A Lorne Simpkins short story)
A Time To Heal (A Sweet Romance)
A Time For Change (A Sweet Romance)
High Spirits
The Temptation series (Romantic Suspense/New Adult Novellas)
Past Temptation
Lost Temptation

KEEP IN TOUCH WITH THE AUTHOR:

Twitter

https://twitter.com/Melcom1

Blog

http://melcomley.blogspot.com

Facebook

http://smarturl.it/sps7jh

Newsletter

http://smarturl.it/8jtcvv

BookBub

www.bookbub.com/authors/m-a-comley

ACKNOWLEDGMENTS

A special thank you to my dear friend, Noelle Holten, for sharing her expert advice to write certain parts of this book.

Thank you as always to my rock, Jean, I'd be lost without you in my life.

Special thanks as always go to my talented editor Stefanie Spangler Buswell and to Karri Klawiter for her superb cover design expertise.

My heartfelt thanks go to my wonderful proofreader Joseph for spotting all the lingering nits.

M A Comley

PROLOGUE

Ten years ago...

Aisha Thomas stepped through the front gate of her semi-detached Thetford home just after five thirty. She was back from work earlier than normal as she had made plans to go out to the theatre with a couple of girlfriends she hadn't seen in a while. Flake, her one-eyed black rescue cat, greeted her at the front door. She swooped him into her arms and snuggled her face into his fur. "Have you missed me, baby?"

Flake's purring was all the response she needed. She carried her fur baby into the kitchen and placed him on the counter while she opened a can of cat food. "Now don't get in the way. Have some patience for a change."

After dropping a few biscuits into the bowl alongside the tinned meat, she placed the bowl on the floor. Flake jumped down and eagerly started eating.

"Right, I better get ready now, or the girls will string me up." Before going upstairs, Aisha checked to see if there were any messages on the answerphone, or if her husband, Patrick, had left any post for her to open. She found neither and continued up the stairs with a spring in her step, keen to jump in the bath and get ready for her night out.

She opened the wardrobe doors, removed several outfits, and laid them out on the bed before she hopped in the bath for a quick soak. When Aisha returned to the bedroom, a towel wrapped around her torso and another one in a turban around her hair, she thought she heard a noise downstairs. She glanced at the clock—it was too early for her policeman husband to be home. She ignored the noise, thinking it must have been Flake. He was a clumsy cat and frequently knocked things off shelves due to his limited vision.

Aisha sat down at the dressing table, ruffled her long black hair with the towel, and began to dry it with the hairdryer. Not until she had finished did she sense someone was watching her. She swivelled on the dralon-covered stool and gasped.

"What? What are you doing here?"

The masked intruder rushed forward, grabbed her by the hair, and forced her onto the carpeted floor. "Lie there and don't move," the gruff voice ordered, muffled by the balaclava.

"Please don't hurt me. I have money I can give you—not much but enough—if you'll let me go."

"Shut up." The intruder paced the floor, scratching nervously at his mask.

"What do you need? I have to go out soon."

"You ain't going nowhere, bitch. Now shut up, let me think."

Aisha swallowed the bile that had lodged in her throat. She had no idea what to do for the best—lie there in silence as instructed, or attempt to negotiate a way out of the situation? She pulled the towel tighter around her, covering her slim legs. *Keep calm! Just listen and do what the person says, then I might get out of this alive.*

The intruder continued to pace the floor, agitation, increasing their speed.

Aisha looked over at the door to see Flake standing there. "Go, Flake, get out of here."

The intruder swiftly pounced on the cat, wrapping their hands around Flake's neck.

"Please, he's done nothing. Let him go. You're scaring him."

Flake squealed, scratched the assailant's hand, and managed to wriggle free.

"Run, Flake, run." Aisha heard the cat run down the stairs and out through the catflap, leaving her alone with the intruder.

"He might have escaped, but don't think you'll do the same."

"What do you want from me? My husband will be home soon. Take what you want and leave."

"Stop giving me orders." The intruder stepped forward and slapped her around the face.

Blood started to pour from her lip. The metallic taste seeped into her mouth, and she held her hand over the wound, staring up at her assailant. "Please... why are you doing this? Give me a reason."

"I don't need a *reason*. I told you to be quiet. Let me think."

"About what? If you're having to think about being here, then that proves you really don't want to pursue this situation. Let me go, and I promise not to say anything."

"You won't get a chance to say anything." The intruder withdrew a knife and flicked their thumb against the blade.

Aisha shuffled back towards the bed, her gaze drawn to the blade as her mouth dried up.

"You mentioned money—where do you keep it?"

"My husband and I keep a couple hundred pounds tucked away in the drawer over there for emergencies."

"Ha, you could say this is an emergency." Keeping one eye on her, the masked person moved backwards towards the drawer she had pointed at. They rummaged around, withdrew a wad of notes, and fanned them. "That'll do for starters. What about jewellery? Where do you keep it?"

Aisha's hand trembled as she pointed to the small drawer in the middle of the dressing table. "In there. There are some valuable pieces that I've inherited from my family."

Yanking open the drawer, the intruder began stuffing the jewellery in their pocket. Then walked back towards Aisha, the person's pace slow and full of intent.

"I have nothing else," she pleaded, clutching the towel.

"Then my work is done here." The intruder grabbed her arm and yanked her to her feet.

She clawed and tried to bite the person. Her assailant sank their teeth into her arm in retaliation before the knife sliced her throat. The movement happened so quickly that Aisha didn't get the chance to defend herself. Her attacker pushed Aisha away, and she fell in a heap to the floor. The excruciating pain coming from her throat worried her. Her hand instinctively covered the gaping wound, and she felt the sticky blood seeping through her fingers. She looked her assailant in the eye and found the strength to say one word before she slumped to the floor as the darkness overcame her. "Why?"

CHAPTER ONE

Detective Inspector Sally Parker of the Norfolk Constabulary arrived at work as the hands on the incident room wall clock hit eight thirty. She had left home early to avoid being snarled up by the roadworks hampering her route into work. *Better to be safe than sorry, girl.*

"Morning, Joanna. You're early this morning. How come?"

"Morning, boss. I thought I'd come in early to tie up a few loose ends on the Morgan case."

"Boy, was I glad to see the back of that case. He was a sly bloody fox, wasn't he?" Sally asked the young detective constable.

"He was, ma'am. It's surprising just how many of these cases end up with the same result, the husband killing the wife."

Sally nodded and walked into her office as the memories she tried to suppress came flooding back. She shook her head, refusing to live through the ordeal yet again. She did enough of that in her bed at night and didn't need to relive the experiences during the day, as well. However, sometimes a domestic violence case cropped up for her team and caused her to revisit her punishing past all over again. She had to admit that although the pain was subsiding, she still flinched when she encountered a certain type of man—such as their last suspect. Instinct had told her not to trust the man as soon as she'd interviewed him. But it had still been a shock to discover he was the one who had killed his wife and disposed of her body in that well on his friend's farm. He'd tried to lay the blame on his friend, but the DNA evidence gathered at the scene disproved his claim and pointed firmly in his direction. That was when Sally saw the similarities between Morgan and her ex-husband—both were suave and sophisticated until pushed into a corner, and that was when the masks slipped.

Thankfully, Darryl was serving time as his punishment for raping her. It had taken all her strength and courage to speak out in court. People were under the illusion that type of thing wasn't supposed to happen to strong coppers. But it did. Since her revelation, Sally had received numerous e-mails from serving female police officers who had found themselves in the same heartbreaking situation, trapped in senselessly violent marriages. Her courage had given them the bravery to lay charges against their own husbands or partners, in some cases. That had made Sally feel proud and far from alone. It had also confirmed that she was right to speak out about her problems living with an abusive partner. Her parents had supported her decision, too. They'd been in the dark up until then and had no idea of the living hell that had entrapped her for years. They had thought the sun shone out of Darryl's backside until she had sat them down and relayed what the evil man had put her through.

The phone on her desk shrilled, pulling her away from her bad memories. She rushed around the desk and flopped into her chair. "Hello. DI Parker. How can I help?"

"Inspector, I'd like to see you in my office immediately." Sally recognised her DCI's officious voice instantly.

"I'll be there right away, sir." But she was listening to the dial tone. *He's so damn rude!* She marched out of her office.

Joanna looked up as Sally swept past her. "Where's the fire, boss?"

"Up my arse. I've been summoned. Be back soon."

Joanna chuckled.

Hmm... no laughing matter for me, I can tell you.

DCI Mick Green's door was open when she arrived. She rapped on it and stuck her head around the doorframe. "All right to come in, sir?"

"Of course. Take a seat, Parker."

Sally sat opposite him, her hands clutched in her lap. She smiled briefly and asked, "Have I done something wrong, sir?"

"I don't know. Have you? Why is that always the first question out of your mouth when I summon you?"

She shrugged. "Natural reaction, I suppose. I can't think of anything that I've done wrong."

"Good. One less thing for me to worry about." He picked up the blue folder in front of him and threw it over the desk towards her. It skidded across the surface and landed in her lap.

She caught the folder before its contents tipped on the floor. Sally placed the folder on the desk and flipped it open. Then she looked up at him. "It's not one of my cases, sir."

He tutted, his annoyance evident. "I'm well aware of that, Inspector. It's going to be yours from now on. It's a cold case from ten years ago. I want you to reinvestigate it for me."

"Any specific reason, sir?"

"Does there have to be a specific reason other than this station never likes to leave a case unsolved?"

"But why now? Why ten years later?"

He tutted again. "If you flip to the back page, which has been updated in the last few days, you'll find out."

Sally flicked through the pages and read the final sentence, then her gaze met his once more. Frowning, she asked, "New DNA evidence has surfaced?"

"Indeed. The culprits were always thought to be two burglars who had carried out a number of burglaries around the time of Aisha Thomas's death. However, those two burglars' bodies have now been uncovered at a building site out in Thetford. During the post-mortem, a sample of DNA was found in the deceased's mouth. Apparently, the pathologist assumed that the deceased had bitten her attacker before she had passed away. He also assumed that the culprit had tried to remove that DNA from the deceased's mouth before he left the crime scene. However, the perpetrator still left behind a bite mark which can be matched to dental records."

"If the SIO at the time attributed the crime to these burglars then why weren't they arrested?"

"By the looks of things, they were both killed around the same time as Aisha Thomas. So, in fact, I'm handing over a cold case which involves three unsolved murders, not just one. They might be connected; they might not. Any objections, Inspector?"

Sally shook her head. "Not at all, sir. It seems a complex case, one that could take a long time to solve. How long have I got?"

"I'll give you a month."

Sally's eyes bulged. "A month? Is that open to be extended?"

"We'll see. Report back to me at every opportunity as usual."

Cold Case

"And you want my whole team working on this, or are there man-hour constraints on this one, sir?"

"Your whole team. You can work other crimes as they come in. If a major crime comes up, then we will reassess the situation. How does that sound to you?"

"Doable, I suppose. I'll get on it right away, sir."

"Good. Close the door on your way out."

Sally rose from her chair and exited the room. A sinking feeling settled in her stomach. She would spend the next couple of hours looking through the file, making notes about what had happened and what the investigating officers had neglected to follow up on, before she involved her team.

The rest of the team had arrived at their desks in her absence. "Morning, all. We've got an interesting cold case ahead of us today. Let me read through it first, and I'll bring you up to speed in an hour or two at the most. Until then, finish off any cases you've been dealing with. We're still going to have to deal with the day-to-day stuff, but the DCI wants this case to get priority for the next month or so."

"Wow, he's given us a whole month to solve it? That's generous of him," her partner Jack Blackman said, his tone laced with sarcasm.

"Yep, possible extension might be considered if we're close to cracking the case. I wouldn't hold my breath on that one, though." Sally grabbed a cup of coffee from the vending machine and walked into the office, closing the door behind her.

The next few hours consisted of her mostly shaking her head and making copious notes. She finally emerged from her office to consult her team. "Gather around, ladies and gents." As she spoke, she entered the details of the case and pinned the relevant photos onto the incident board. "Okay, this is what we have. Our victim is thirty-year-old Aisha Thomas. She was a talented music teacher at the local comprehensive school. Here's the interesting fact about this case: she was also married to one of our own."

The team began to murmur. "Is the husband still a copper now, boss?" Detective Constable Jordan Reid asked.

"That's something we'll need to check on, Jordan. Do that for me after this meeting. He'll need to be questioned."

Jordan made a note on his pad.

"Obvious question if I may, boss," Joanna said. "You say it's a cold case... why are we investigating it now?"

"I'm coming to that, Joanna. On the evening of the killing, according to the report, the husband, Patrick Thomas, came home from work at around seven, saw his wife's bag on the kitchen worktop, and went upstairs to look for her. His wife was supposed to be going out with friends that evening, so he presumed she was getting ready. When he walked into the bedroom, he found her lying on the carpet. Her throat had been sliced open, and there was blood all around her. He ended up with blood on his hands as he tried to save her, but it was too late."

"Do you think that was set up as a distraction for the investigating officers, boss?" Joanna asked.

"That's what we need to find out. Instinct always kicks in at times like these. I defy anyone in this room who, upon discovering a loved one with a fatal wound, would not offer any form of assistance."

Several team members nodded their agreement.

"That being said, we still shouldn't discount the fact he's a possible suspect. I'll know more once I've interviewed him. It'll be interesting to see if he moved on with his life quickly or is still left in limbo after all these years. Going back to the question of why this case has been presented to us, well, the two main suspects were believed to be burglars ransacking the neighbourhood around that time. Their bodies were discovered recently in a shallow grave on a building site on the edge of Thetford Forest."

Jack shook his head and shrugged. "You've lost me. I'm still not seeing where this is leading, boss."

"It's complex, so bear with me. Once the forensic evidence results came back and matched to their names, this case was highlighted as being unsolved. The victim, Aisha Thomas had a bite mark on her arm, presumably left by her murderer. That bite mark was compared to the dental records of the burglars, but instead of coming back positive, both men were instantly exonerated."

"Ah, I see. What about the husband? Could he have bitten his wife? Maybe during a sex session?" Jack asked.

"That's yet another thing we have to delve into."

Joanna raised her hand to speak, and Sally nodded for her to go ahead. "Were there any other suspects at the time of the crime, boss?"

"Not really. Once they discounted the husband, the investigating officers turned their attention to the two burglars. Now that has been disproven, we're going to have to start from scratch again."

"Ten years later? What if people have moved away from the area?" Jack asked.

"Then we'll just have to track them down, Jack. That's never been a problem for us before. We can call on other forces to help us out on that, I suppose. Like I've stated already, we've been given a limited time to solve this case. We'll be reliant on others lending a hand."

"So, where do you want us to begin, boss?" Joanna asked with a frown.

It was the first time her team had been asked to deal with a cold case, and she could tell by the questions they were asking that they were already out of their depth. "Let's get one thing straight: we should forget this is a cold case. Let's treat it as a new case; it'll be less restricting for us. So, let's start from the beginning. I'll leave the file on the desk for you all to look at. There's a list of people Aisha was associated to in there. We need to go through that list meticulously. Obviously, the first person I need to speak with will be the husband. We'll work through the list together and make notes on the board if anything crops up linked to the case. Let's see if we can wrap this up sooner than the DCI expects. Let's get cracking team. Keep me up to date with things as the investigation progresses."

The team got back to work as Sally finished off adding a few notes to the incident board. Seconds later, Jordan appeared beside her.

"Boss, Patrick Thomas is still a serving constable at this station."

"He is? Have you ever run into him?"

Jordan's mouth turned down at the side, and he shrugged. "Can't say I've come across him myself, boss. Anyway, he's on duty at present. Do you want me to arrange a meeting with him?"

"It might be a good idea for me to chat with his immediate superior first, get a gist of what his mental state has been like since the crime took place."

"Want me to get the sergeant on the phone for you?"

"Yep. Let me get back to my office then pass the call through. Thanks, Jordan."

CHAPTER TWO

Sally rushed back into her office, taking her notes with her. The phone rang a few seconds later. "Hello?"

"I have Sergeant Potts on the line for you, boss."

"Thanks, Jordan." She paused until she heard the click of Jordan hanging up. "Hello, Sergeant Potts?"

"That's right, Inspector. What can I do for you?"

"I wanted a confidential word with you before I interview a member of your staff."

"That sounds ominous, ma'am. May I ask who?"

Sally cleared her throat. "Constable Patrick Thomas. I've been instructed to investigate his wife's murder case."

"Blimey, after all these years? It's probably none of my business, but can I ask why, ma'am?"

"New evidence has been uncovered, shedding doubt on the validity of the original investigation, primarily the suspects. What I really want to know is how Constable Thomas has been since his wife's death."

He sighed heavily. "At the time, her death hit him very hard, as you can imagine, ma'am. However, over the years, he's learned to accept it. Always been the type to throw himself into his work to forget his woes, and who can blame him? It's not good to wallow in self-pity over things like this. No point to it. I'm sure you'll agree."

"I understand. Okay, would you mind if I meet up with him today for an informal interview?"

"Not at all. Would you like me to send him along to you now, ma'am?"

"Excellent. I'll have to do it in the interview room downstairs, where the recording equipment is. He won't be intimidated by that, will he?"

"I shouldn't think so, ma'am. He'll appreciate these things have to be done properly. In ten minutes, okay?"

"Perfect, thanks, Sergeant." Sally hung up and quickly checked through the post lying on her desk, ignoring anything not marked *urgent*. After dealing with a few enquiries and jotting down quick replies, she left her office and dropped by Jack's desk. "I'm off to interview Thomas. Do you want to be in on this one?"

He stood up. "Might as well hear it from the horse's mouth."

"Everything all right at home, Jack?" Sally asked as they made their way downstairs.

"I take it you're referring to how Teresa is dealing with her baby?"

Sally smiled. "Unless there's anything else you're keeping from me?"

"Nah, that's enough to be getting on with. The baby is fine—teething, so keeping us awake most of the night. Other than that, Mary Rose is just fine." In spite of his complaints about his grandchild, his face always lit up when he spoke about her.

"How old is she now?" Sally stepped off the bottom stair and turned the corner to the interview rooms.

"Almost two. Time flies, doesn't it?"

Sally turned to face him. "Wow, really? That has gone quick. She's worth it, though, right?"

"Yeah, even though I was made a grandpa far before my time."

Sally smiled and opened the door to the interview room. Constable Thomas rose from his chair when they walked in. "There's no need to stand on ceremony. Take a seat, Patrick." She extended her hand for him to shake and sat down opposite. "I don't think we've met before. I'm DI Sally Parker of CID, and this is my partner, DS Jack Blackman."

"Pleased to meet you, ma'am. Have I done something wrong?"

Sally shook her head and offered a smile. "No. This is tough for me to tell you, but my team has been handed your wife's murder case to reopen."

His eyes widened, and his mouth dropped open before he regained his composure. "Can I ask why, ma'am? It's been ten years since..."

"We've uncovered new evidence which questions the original investigators' main two suspects. I'm sorry if this will cause you any discomfort, but I'm going to have to ask you to recount the events of what happened that day."

He puffed out his cheeks. "I haven't thought about that side of things in years, ma'am. Of course, I think about Aisha constantly, although I try to block out the images of finding her bloody body in our bedroom." His eyes misted up with genuine grief.

"We're going to be working through the list of possible suspects, but I just wanted to know if you had an inkling who could be behind her death. Maybe someone you know has acted differently towards you since that day?"

"That's like asking me if the sun ever rises in the morning, ma'am, because everyone I know acted strangely around me at the time. People do when they don't know how to handle someone who's grieving. It's human nature."

"That's true. I suppose what I'm asking is if anyone has acted or done anything out of the ordinary towards you that really sticks out. Did anyone cut you off perhaps?"

He placed his hand around his chin and pondered her question for a moment. "Not that I can think of. I'm grateful that all my friends appeared to stick by me, if I'm honest. I'm not sure I would have treated someone the same way if the boot was on the other foot. Maybe that's more about me being a copper and having a suspicious mind."

Sally studied the man as he spoke. According to the notes she'd just read, he was nearing forty. He had a few grey hairs showing just above his ears. He was thin, almost to the point of emaciation. When he'd stood up to greet her, Sally's overall impression of him was that he was still suffering emotionally and physically because of his wife's death. Of course, guilt was a probable cause for that. He probably blamed himself for not arriving home sooner to save her— or was he guilty of actually taking his wife's life? Her gut instinct was for the former scenario. "Did you return to work soon after the incident occurred?"

"Yes, ma'am. I had to. I was going out of my mind going over things at home."

"Do you still live at the same address?"

"That's right. Although, I can't bear to go in the master bedroom anymore. I moved into the smaller spare room. I should sell up and move on, but that would mean the culprit has won. Staying in the house gives me the connection I need to be near Aisha." He sighed and stared at the table for a second. "It was our first home together. I still feel her presence in the house. Sorry if that makes me sound a bit loopy."

Sally smiled at him. "It doesn't. Perhaps you *should* consider moving."

"In the very beginning, I thought about letting the house go, but the cost implications would have been too much for me to bear. I don't make much being a constable, as you can appreciate, ma'am. It's an expensive business to keep moving. We bought that house because it was in a nice neighbourhood—well, it *was* until all those burglaries started to take place."

"I understand totally. I need to discuss the forensic evidence that has come to light. You're aware that the murderer bit your wife's arm?"

"Yes, ma'am. I was the one who pointed that out when the pathologist arrived at the house."

"Well, it's come to our attention that there is no way the two burglars in question could have killed your wife, as the bite marks don't tally with either their skeletal remains or their dental records."

"I don't understand, ma'am. Skeletal remains? You mean their bodies have been discovered?"

"Yes, in a shallow grave on a building site close to the forest in Thetford."

He scratched his head. "So that would indicate that they've been dead a few years. Is that right, ma'am?"

"Yes, I've yet to speak to the pathologist dealing with the case, but it would appear so."

"Ah, now I understand why the case has to be reopened. I'm at a loss to think who could have killed Aisha if these men have been exonerated. But surely the investigating officer would have matched the bite mark to the dental records of these two during the case, wouldn't he?"

"Obviously not. Otherwise, the two men would have been discounted instantly."

"That's unthinkable, ma'am," he stated, looking genuinely perturbed.

"It's deplorable. Something I'm keen to put right. Moving on, back then, did you supply a list of friends and family for the investigators to question?" Sally had seen only a few people on the list—too few, considering Aisha was a music teacher.

"I did. We didn't really have that many friends."

"What about family? Did Aisha come from a big family? Did she have a lot of extended family members we can speak to?"

"Aisha had a large family. She was Muslim, her parents from Pakistan. Some of them have moved away from the area, I believe. They cut me off as soon as Aisha was buried."

"Why? Because they suspected you of killing her?"

Patrick's gaze dropped to the table, and he shrugged. "I could never get a proper answer from them. They didn't actually come out and say the words, but the inference was there that either they blamed me for killing her or at least blamed me for not protecting her as I should have done. Their culture is totally different to ours, ma'am. I did my best to provide for Aisha, however, it was never good enough in their eyes. They were furious that she married a Christian. Aisha didn't care—she loved me for who I was, not for the religion I followed, but her parents simply didn't get it. I'm not one to slag people off, ma'am, but it might be better if you spoke to them about how they felt regarding our marriage, because they barely spoke to me unless Aisha was in the room."

"I'm sorry, Patrick. At the time, you would have needed their support to deal with your wife's death, not their animosity." He nodded his agreement. "It's an avenue we will be investigating, I promise you. Can you think back to any work-related issues you might have had around that time?"

He frowned. "I'm sorry, ma'am, in what way?"

"Perhaps you made an arrest and someone threatened you? Said they were going to get retribution by harming your family, something along those lines?"

He fell silent for a while as he thought. "I'm at a loss to remember that far back, ma'am. I'm sure if there had been something around that time, it would have stuck in my mind, but there's nothing. She was such a lovely girl, caring, compassionate, eager to help others.

That's why her death—and the way it had occurred—shook me up so much." His hands covered his face for a few seconds before he wiped away a tear. "That image of seeing her lying there with her beautiful throat cut will haunt me forever. When I close my eyes at night, it's the last thing I see, and when I wake up in the morning, it's the first image that fills my mind. There's no escaping it. I can only describe it as a living nightmare. I know that sounds like a cliché, but there's just no other way to describe it, ma'am."

"I totally understand. I went through a horrendous personal ordeal, and it affects me in pretty much the same way. Have you had any form of counselling, Patrick?"

"They offered it to me, ma'am, but I would have felt a wuss had I accepted. I've learnt to cope with things myself over the years. Yes, there are good days and bad days, but on the whole, I've learnt how to keep my emotions in check. Even if that means I go through life on autopilot occasionally, it has been my coping mechanism over the years."

"But how long will you give it? Before you move on with your life, I mean."

"How long is that proverbial piece of string, ma'am? The heart doesn't heal as quickly when someone you love dearly has been stolen from you in such a cruel way. I'll get there one day, I guess."

"I hope for your sake that day comes swiftly, Patrick. Can you do me a favour and try and list all Aisha's friends and family? Just in case you forgot to mention anyone at the time of the original investigation. This isn't an exercise of trying to trip you up, I promise. Your mind might be a little clearer than it was immediately after Aisha's death."

"Do you want me to do that now, ma'am, or this evening after work?"

"This evening or over the next few days will do. Maybe if you still have Aisha's possessions, you'll be able to lay your hand on her address book, if she had one at the time."

He nodded, his brow furrowed. "I know where that is. I have it tucked away in a keepsake box in the wardrobe. I only looked through it the other day. It would have been our twelfth wedding anniversary this week."

"I'm sorry. I had no idea. Let's call this meeting to a halt then. If you can bring that information to me in my office in the next day or two, I'd appreciate it."

"I'll do it for you tonight without fail, ma'am."

Sally rose from her chair, and Jack and Patrick joined her as she made her way over to the door. She entered the hallway to find a tall, redheaded female constable standing with her back against the wall.

The woman glanced at Sally with a concerned expression.

"Constable? May I help you?"

Her cheeks coloured up. "Sorry, ma'am, I was waiting for Constable Thomas. I'm his partner."

"Ah, I see. He's free to join you now."

The woman smiled and looked over Sally's shoulder at Patrick. "We've had a call we need to attend urgently."

Sally stepped aside to allow Patrick to pass then watched Patrick and the woman rush up the hallway together and out of the station.

"What's your gut telling you on this one, boss?" Jack asked on their walk back to the incident room.

"That he's a sad, lonely man who has never got over the death of his wife. Whether that's related to his guilt in killing her..." She shook her head. "It's hard to say at this point. He seemed genuine enough to me. I didn't spot any chinks in his emotional story, did you?"

"Nope, it all seems hunky-dory to me. So, where do we go from here?"

"I'm not willing to move on just yet. Tomorrow, I want to hear what his partner has to say. Let's check how long they've been partners first. There's no point questioning her if she's only just teamed up with him. If they've been together for a long time, there's a chance he might have shared some strange secret with her—loose lips and all that."

"I'm with you. I have to add a word of caution to that idea: that's only likely if the partners get on, boss. If they hate working with each other, then they're hardly going to share deep, dark secrets," Jack said.

They reached the top of the stairs and entered the incident room.

Sally clapped her hands to gain the team's attention. "We've just interviewed the husband. It went okay, nothing spectacular to report. He's going to furnish us with a list of friends and relatives that we should speak to. Until we have that, we'll just have to work with what we've already got at our disposal. Anyone have anything else they wish to add?"

"We were talking amongst ourselves when you left, boss, and Joanna came up with an idea that maybe we should look into," Jordan stated, turning to look at Joanna.

Sally raised an expectant eyebrow at Joanna. "I'm listening and open to anything at this stage. What did you have in mind?"

"It might be totally off the wall, boss, but it is something that is becoming more prevalent within Muslim culture."

Sally perched on the edge of the desk behind her and folded her arms, the way she always did when something intrigued her. "Don't stop there, Joanna. Come on, speak freely."

"I need to do more research into the subject, boss, but I think we should consider maybe this being some form of honour killing."

Sally's eyes widened, and Jack, who was sitting back at his desk, almost choked on his cup of coffee. "Seriously? What has led you to think along those lines, Joanna?" Sally asked.

"I apologise if I've spoken out of turn, but something resonated with me regarding a case I read about in the paper last month. This happened up north, Bradford way; it might be different up there, boss."

"Can you fill us all in on the story?"

"I can give you the gist of it, boss. I can't tell you the ins and outs of it, however."

Sally nodded and motioned for Joanna to continue.

"From what I can remember, a young Muslim woman married a white British man against her parents' wishes. They refused to go to her wedding, even refused to acknowledge the marriage had taken place. Apparently, her father had made arrangements for his daughter to marry a wealthy businessman back in Pakistan, but the girl fell in love with the man whom she had married. Her parents were shocked, didn't even know the couple were seeing one another. The announcement they'd secretly eloped had almost killed the girl's mother; she ended up in hospital needing a heart operation."

"That's not good. So, what happened next?"

"The husband of the young woman—I've forgotten her name, sorry—he reported her as a missing person one day. He suspected her family had something to do with her disappearance all along, but the police had trouble finding evidence to back up his theory."

"Okay, so how did the truth emerge?" Sally asked, shaking her head in confusion.

Joanna looked her in the eye. "The family insisted that the daughter had made a mistake, that she didn't love her husband anymore and pleaded for their forgiveness. They said they had sent their daughter back to Pakistan to stay with relatives. But the leading investigator had a hard time believing the father, especially as he couldn't find the girl's name listed on any flights that had left the UK since her disappearance."

"How naïve do these people think we are? Go on."

"The policeman followed the girl's mother one day to a site in the woods and watched the woman leave a single white rose on the forest floor underneath a large oak tree. She sat on the ground and sobbed. Once the mother left the area, he called a forensic team to the site, and that's when the young woman's body was discovered. Both her parents were arrested and charged with her murder, along with the father's brother, who actually admitted he was the one who killed his niece."

"My God, how barbaric. It seems bizarre that this type of thing can happen in this country. How stupid of the family not to think that the British police would trace the body of the victim eventually."

"Apparently, there are numerous honour killings that take place on British soil, boss. I can't think of the statistics right now, but I was shocked when I read what it was. I can do some checking for you."

"Yes, do that, Joanna. This is something that we truly shouldn't dismiss, especially as I've just heard Patrick and her parents had a strained relationship. I don't remember seeing any mention of the original investigation going down that route ten years ago. Maybe the investigator didn't have any reason to suspect the family, or perhaps it wasn't something he was willing to consider back then. Let's delve into this further. I think we should go and see the parents, Jack, if only to put this theory to bed. But if we go in there forearmed about this bizarre ceremonious act this culture is willing to bring to our shores, it might just catch the parents off guard."

"Just a thought, boss... is the investigating officer still around?" Jack asked.

Sally shrugged. "I'm not sure. Can you look into that for me? See what sort of record he had for solving cases? Let's hit this case from all angles, shake the tree a little, and see what falls out, eh?"

She walked into her office, her stomach all of a sudden tied into large knots. Sally sat behind her desk and picked up the phone. "It's me. Is it all right if I pop round this evening?"

"I'd love that. As it happens, I'm pretty clear this afternoon. Do you want to come straight from work?"

"Would you mind? I'll give Mum a ring, tell her not to expect me home tonight."

"That's a little presumptuous of you. Not that I'm complaining."

"Didn't think you would. See you around six."

She ended the call with a huge smile on her face and thousands of butterflies in her stomach chasing the knots away.

CHAPTER THREE

Sally was smiling inwardly as she opened the gate to the large detached house in Attleborough and rang the doorbell. She leaned against the wall until the door opened. A hand shot out, latched on to her arm, and pulled her into the hallway. Simon's mouth quickly covered hers, and she melted into his arms. She groaned as his kiss deepened and his hands began to wander. Sally turned her head away and pushed at his chest.

"Slow down, lover boy."

"Why? There's no fun in that."

Sally ducked under Simon's arm and ran up the long hallway into the kitchen, where she began inspecting the pots sitting on the stove. "What's for dinner? I'm starving."

"So was I, but as that's off the menu, I suppose pork chops and dauphinoise potatoes will have to do instead."

Sashaying towards him, she pouted. "Aww... don't be like that. I have some business I need to discuss with you before we... well, you know."

He placed a hand over his chest. "What? You mean to tell me that you haven't come over here to use and abuse my body? I'm mortified."

She laughed. "Anyone ever tell you that you've missed your vocation? You should be plying your trade in a different theatre, on the stage, instead of cutting up bodies for a living."

"Ha, I'd probably get paid more being a comedian than a pathologist. I wouldn't get as many perks, though."

"What bloody perks?"

"I get to see you during the day, sometimes."

"Ah, there is that. Plus, I come over a few nights a week for bed and breakfast."

"Nice to know I have my uses. Dinner will be ready in five minutes."

"Hmm... so you really had no intention of whisking me upstairs to bed the minute I arrived anyway, did you?"

He held his hands up. "I've been rumbled. I'm starving, too. We should eat first and then see where the evening takes us."

Sally stepped closer and kissed his cheek. "Want to talk business now, or do you need to concentrate? I know how much you men hate multi-tasking."

He glared at her for an instant, but his scowl diminished quickly. "I'm neither confirming nor denying that statement, but I would like some peace and quiet while I serve up. You can help by laying the table if you would."

"I think I can manage that."

Five minutes later, with the table laid and the food sitting on the white plates in front of them, they chinked their glasses together. "To us," Simon announced.

"To us. It might have taken us a few years to get together, but I'm thankful we finally came to our senses. My mate Lorne would be proud of us."

"She knew something was going to happen between us before we did. Is she always that intuitive?"

"Yep, she goes a lot by gut feelings, that one, and I have to say she's not often wrong. I love her to bits. It's a shame she and Tony don't live closer. Maybe they'll be tempted to retire this way in the future. Hark at me, talking about retirement. Mind you, I suppose she's getting on a bit."

Simon shook his head. "I'm going to let that comment slip past because I remember you telling me that Lorne and I are of a similar age."

"That's right, unlike me. I'm still in the prime of my life at thirty-one."

"I'm hardly ancient at forty-four. I bet I could outrun you over a short distance."

"Not doubting that, but I bet your stamina to go the extra mile is questionable."

"You're just full of bloody compliments tonight, aren't you? Right, let's talk about business before I make up the spare room for you."

Sally winked at him. "It'll be your loss, honey. Not mine."

"I don't believe that for a second. Come on, let me have it—the case, I mean."

Sally ate the last mouthful of dinner from her plate, washed it down with a swig of wine then sat back in her chair. "I've been given a cold case to work on. I was going to ring you to ask your opinion during the day but thought I'd wait until this evening."

"That's no problem. Do I know about this case?"

"I'm not sure. In a roundabout way, you might. I was given the file this morning by DCI Green—oh damn, I'm going around in circles here. I think you've been working on the remains of two men, suspected burglars who vanished ten years ago."

He nodded. "I am. Is that the cold case you're referring to?"

"Yes and no. The two men were the suspects in the murder of Aisha Thomas. She was married to one of the constables at the station."

"I can vaguely remember the case. It was before my time, though. I can dig out the file tomorrow if you like."

"That'd be great. I questioned the husband today, and the jury is still out on that one for me. He talked the talk. Not sure if that was his professional mode guiding him, however."

Simon took a sip from his glass as she spoke and then asked, "How can I help?"

"I'm not sure, really. I suppose I would like to bounce some ideas around with you, if you're up for that?"

"Of course, fire away."

"Well, I've yet to talk to the inspector who originally dealt with the case, but it seems he was keen to point the finger at these two burglars who had robbed several homes in the nearby neighbourhood. However, after the murder of Aisha Thomas, those burglaries dried up, and the two men vanished. To me, that sounds a little too convenient. How about you?"

"So, you think these men were scapegoats? I carried out the PMs yesterday and today, and I can tell you that these men were both killed around ten years ago."

"Which fits exactly. Any idea how they were killed? I haven't a clue how the men were discovered. Were they buried in the same grave?"

"Yes, it was a somewhat crude burial. The men were buried on top of each other. The thing is that they were only buried a few feet down, as if the person who dug the grave couldn't be bothered to dig any deeper—or dig a second grave for the other man. Perhaps if they had, the burglars' bodies would have remained undiscovered."

"Crap, okay, so that tells me that we're not looking at a professional killer at least. They'd never be that sloppy, for a start."

"I'm with you on that one, Sally. How they were killed is going to take a little more time to sort out, as you can imagine. I'm dealing with two sets of bones as opposed to intact bodies with visible wounds to guide me. I'll hopefully have something for you in the next day or two."

"That's okay. We've got enough to be going on with at the moment anyway, looking back over friends' and family's statements. Let me run this past you, if I may?"

He tilted his head. "Shoot."

"The victim was Pakistani and married to a British white male... see where I'm going with this?"

"I think so. Go on."

"A member of my team—Joanna—said that she'd read about a case recently in which a girl marrying outside her religion was killed by her relatives, an honour killing. Have you dealt with any such cases over the years?"

"One or two that were suspected but never proven. The family tend to close ranks on that type of thing. I read about the case you're referring to. I think the mother finally led the investigator to the girl's grave. Am I right?"

Sally nodded.

"It's usually the mothers who suffer from the pangs of guilt the most, in my experience. In their culture, the women have to do what the men say, as though they have no voice. My take on it is that the mother could no longer live with the burden of guilt hanging around her shoulders, and she led the police to the grave."

"I can understand why she would do that. Wouldn't she feel the wrath of the family, though?"

"Yes, but by that time, everyone hopefully would have been arrested and put behind bars."

"But then these families tend to be large. Wouldn't the mother be looking over her shoulder the rest of her life?"

"If I remember rightly, I think the mother must have thought something similar, because she actually ended her own life in the remand centre."

"How dreadful. I wasn't aware of that," Sally replied, astonished.

"Maybe you shouldn't be led down that route, given that the two burglars lost their lives around the same time Aisha died."

"I'll bear that in mind. I still need to question the family, see what comes to light there. Any pudding?"

He laughed at her swift change of subject. "Why are you always thinking of your stomach, and how is it that you manage to stay so slim?"

"My age obviously works in my favour there."

"Cheeky! What are you saying—that middle-age spread is rearing its head in my case?" He rubbed his protruding belly.

"Not at all. Hey, if the cap fits."

"We could always take some ice cream upstairs with us."

Sally found it hard to prevent the shiver travelling down her spine. "I'm up for it, if you are."

"I'll just load the dishwasher."

Sally smiled, forgetting what a cleaning freak he was. Her ex had been the same, however, he had expected *her* to be the one to do the cleaning up. Simon was a different man entirely. Over the past few months, since their relationship had begun, he'd always put her needs before his, at every turn, in and out of the bedroom. He was a caring man, sometimes misunderstood by others. But Sally had no trouble sussing out when he was being serious or pulling her leg. She had to admit, however, that when his accent slipped back into broad Scottish, she had trouble understanding him and resorted to nodding her head, even when she didn't have a clue what he'd said. He had caught her out many a time but laughed it off. He'd never ridiculed her for being lazy—or worse, for being thick, when she didn't understand what he was on about.

Sally had spent her life with Darryl teetering on eggshells most of the time. She was so grateful those days were behind her and that she was now able to enjoy her life. It had taken her a few months to learn to trust Simon, but he understood completely and had waited patiently for her to surrender herself completely to him. Not many men out there would have been prepared to do that, even if they said they were.

Sally watched him prepare a large bowl of ice cream and withdraw two spoons from the kitchen drawer, excitement building inside her.

"Can you make sure the back door is locked, Sal?"

She loved it when he called her that. After checking the back door, they ran upstairs, acting like a pair of teenagers. She couldn't help but feel like a teenager knowing what was about to happen between them.

CHAPTER FOUR

Contented, Sally stretched and stroked her hand over Simon's back. He turned to face her and pulled her close. She felt his erection stirring. "Hey, you, we've both got work today."

"We could pull a sickie," he said with a wink.

Sally kissed him then shot out of bed. "I've never done that in my life, and I don't intend starting now. Is it all right if I hop in the shower?"

His eyes roamed her naked body before he answered, "I could always join you."

"Nice try, Mr. Pathologist. We'd never make it into work."

"It was worth a shot." He rolled over again.

Sally felt a twinge of guilt and was almost tempted to dive back into bed beside him, but one look at the clock swiftly dismissed that notion. She had twenty minutes to shower, get dressed, and leave the house.

When she opened the bathroom door, Simon was leaning against the doorframe, wearing a soppy grin on his face. "Last night was great. We could always make it a permanent thing."

Sally felt the colour rise in her cheeks. It wasn't often she was lost for words.

He closed the gap between them, a look of concern replacing his smile. "If it's too soon... I didn't mean to..."

She touched his face, her hand trembling. "It's not that... well, maybe it is... it's just that I don't want to spoil what we have."

"All right. Hey, forget I said anything."

"Oh no, now I've upset you."

He kissed her gently on the lips. "You've done nothing of the sort. Think it over and get back to me."

"Ugh... that sounds so damn business-like." She laughed, aware that what he'd said had probably come out wrong.

"Sorry, guess I'm not very good at this kind of thing. It's not every day I ask a beautiful young woman to share my house—or my bed, come to that."

"I know it isn't, sweetheart. You know my situation with my parents, though. I'd feel a right shit if I upped and left after only living there a year. There's the mortgage to consider, too."

"You could still continue to pay the mortgage on that place. I wouldn't ask you to contribute here."

"Whoa... what do you take me for? Some kind of gold digger?"

Simon's chin wobbled, and his eyes misted up, which totally threw her.

She had only been joking, but her words had apparently hit him hard. "Hey, Simon, I was joking. Damn, I haven't got time for this. Everything is coming out wrong. Can we have a proper discussion some other time?"

"Of course. You go. I won't be long behind you." He pecked her on the cheek then softly closed the door to the bathroom, his shoulders slumped.

As she dressed, she could hear the shower running. The water was still running five minutes later, when it was time for her to leave. "I'm off now. I'll ring you later," she called out, but he didn't respond.

Sally made her way down the stairs, her legs heavy, and sought out her handbag and keys. She left the house and drove to Wymondham Police Station in a daze, mentally kicking herself for reacting the way she had to Simon's astounding offer. *That's it! I've probably ruined our relationship before it's actually had a chance to get off the ground.*

When she pulled into the car park, Jack was leaning against his car, waiting for her. "Everything all right, boss?"

"Yes, I think so. A personal issue I need to sort out later, that's all."

His eyes narrowed. "I hope that Darryl hasn't been up to his old tricks of causing trouble again."

Sally patted his arm. "No, nothing like that. How are things at home?"

"Same old thing. Didn't get much sleep last night because of the little 'un, but what's new there?"

"Does Teresa get up during the night to tend to the child?"

"Yeah, I can't fault her there. She's definitely doing her bit. Donna and I are getting too old for this shit. We thought we were doing the right thing letting Teresa and her fella move in, but damn, I forgot what it was like having a baby in the house."

"You probably don't want to hear this, but have you thought about asking them to move out?"

"Yeah, Donna and I have pondered doing just that. The thing is, where would they go? The lad is on minimum wage at a factory, and you know the price of renting a flat is through the roof nowadays. What hope is there for them?"

"I hear you. How long are you going to have to put up with sleepless nights, Jack? I know I couldn't do without getting my eight hours sleep a night."

They walked through the station's entrance and up the stairs. "We'll see how we go. Maybe the missus and I just need to get away on holiday for a bit."

"That's not a bad idea. Maybe after we've solved this cold case, you can book some time off."

"Maybe. It's probably not that bad at home really. Just the lack of sleep talking. Where are we going to start today?"

"Let's get a coffee down our necks first, eh?" Sally pushed open the incident room door to find the rest of the team were already at their desks, beavering away. She was lucky to be surrounded by such a conscientious group of officers. "Morning, all. Let me see what dross is filling my desk, and I'll be right with you."

She walked into her office, surveyed the small pile of brown envelopes vying for her attention, and left again. The post could wait, but the cold case couldn't. "Quickest admin slog ever. Where's my coffee, Bullet?" she asked, using the nickname Jack had brought with him from his army days.

He groaned as he stood up and marched across the room to collect a drink from the vending machine. He deposited the cup on the desk beside her and trudged back to his seat.

"Okay, this is what I think we should cover today. We continue to try and trace Aisha's neighbours and friends, plus Jack and I will be going over to see Aisha's parents this morning. I'm not going to ring them. I'll just turn up."

"What about Patrick's partner? Are we going to see what she has to say today, too?" Jack asked.

"Yep, thanks for the reminder. We'll check her shift on the way out with the desk sergeant and call her in for questioning when we return later."

"What about Aisha's place of work, boss? Oh, by the way, Patrick dropped off a list of Aisha's friends. Not many, I'm afraid," Joanna said.

"Can you and Stuart cover the workplace and the friend list, Joanna? Jordan, I'd like you to remain here, searching through the original investigation files, see if anything shows up that we, or the other investigating officer, might have missed."

Sally finished her drink and slipped her coat back on. "Ready, Jack, let's get this over with." He followed her downstairs, where she stopped to speak to the desk sergeant. "Can you tell me if PC Caroline Hawk is on duty today?"

He studied the rota on the wall behind him and nodded. "She's on the day shift, ma'am."

"We're going out to interview the victim's parents now, but I'd like to have a discreet chat with her—preferably without her partner knowing about it—sometime this afternoon."

"About two, ma'am?"

"Sounds perfect to me. Thanks, Sergeant."

Sally and Jack continued out to Sally's car. "We'll go in mine today. I'll leave you to deal with the sat nav."

Jack fell into the passenger seat and punched in the address. "Fifteen minutes."

~ ~ ~

Sally halted the car outside a modest terraced house in a tree-lined street in Snetterton. It seemed a pleasant enough neighbourhood. The houses all seemed as if people took pride in their surroundings, and that was becoming a rarity these days. "Here we go. Not sure what type of reception we'll get, but keep calm, Jack."

He placed a hand over his chest. "Me? I never fly off the handle."

Sally raised her eyebrows and shook her head at the ex-soldier. "If you say so."

She locked the car. Then seconds later, she rang the doorbell to the pebble-dashed house.

A woman wearing a long dress over trousers, with a hijab covering her head, all in monochrome black, opened the door. "Hello, can I help you?"

"Mrs. Maqsood? I'm DI Sally Parker, and this is my partner, DS Jack Blackman. Would it be possible for us to come in and speak with you for a moment or two?"

"In connection with what?" the woman asked, shuffling behind the door.

"We'd rather discuss that inside than on the doorstep," Sally insisted.

The woman left her hiding place and opened the inner door to the house. "Come through to the kitchen. Please remove your shoes first," she called over her shoulder.

Sally and Jack slipped off their shoes then followed the woman through the narrow hallway and past the lounge, which was cluttered with an array of chairs in different sizes and colours. In the dated kitchen at the rear, the woman said, "I have to continue preparing flat breads. Hope you don't mind."

"Please do. Is your husband at home?"

"No. Why do you need to know that? Please tell me what this is about?"

Sally and Jack sat down at the small kitchen table. Jack withdrew his notebook as Sally began to ask the questions. "Mrs. Maqsood, this visit concerns your daughter's death."

The woman looked up at them. "What? I don't understand. My beautiful daughter died over ten years ago. Why are you making enquiries about that now?"

"Because new evidence has come into our hands, and we can't just ignore it."

Mrs. Maqsood's eyes closed and tears dripped onto her cheeks. She shook her head and stopped pulling the dough apart. "What new evidence?" she finally asked after a few quiet seconds.

"Before I tell you that, I'd like to ask you to go over the events surrounding your daughter's death. I appreciate how difficult that may be for you, but it's something we need to hear from you."

"My husband should be here... I can't go through this without him being here."

"If you need your husband with you, then we'll have to ask you both to come down to the station to be questioned separately."

"I don't understand—why? Are you saying you aren't going to believe me?"

"No, it's how we have to obtain a statement. So that your husband cannot influence what you're going to tell us."

She shook her head in disbelief. "You think I would lie about something so precious? About how my daughter perished?"

Damn, this isn't going to plan. "No, it's procedure. I'm sorry if that has offended you. It's more a case of piecing things together. If we obtain statements from people separately, then it might lead us to something that one person has overlooked. Please don't look at it as though we're trying to trip you up."

"How do you expect either of us to remember every single detail that happened ten years ago? Surely you have our original statements. Can you not read through those?"

"We have, and we could do that. However, as the leading investigator on the case, I've made the call to start afresh, just in case the other leading investigator missed something vital."

"Then am I to believe that you have very little trust for this other investigator?"

"No, not at all. It's just that the investigation took a route that this new evidence has now put a degree of doubt to."

"Can you tell me what the new evidence is, or is that a secret?"

Noting the sarcastic tone in the woman's voice, Sally smiled. "I'd rather not say at this point. Can you tell me how you learned of your daughter's death?"

"Patrick called us after the ambulance removed my daughter's body from their home. He should have called me sooner."

"Did you get on with your son-in-law?"

"Yes."

"Do you still see Patrick?"

"No."

"May I ask why not?"

"It's personal."

Sally sighed. "It would help us form a picture if you could explain why."

"He should have saved her."

"But he was on duty, wasn't he?"

"What does that matter? The house should have been made secure. There was no alarm on the property. *We* have an alarm."

"Does the alarm make you feel safe in your own home?"

"Yes."

"And when was the alarm fitted?"

"After my daughter's death."

"Up until that time, you felt safe in your home. Is that right?"

"Yes. I didn't want what happened to Aisha to happen to me."

"That's understandable. What I can't fathom is why you would think that was intentional on his part. Can you enlighten me? Was their marriage in trouble?"

Mrs. Maqsood fell silent. "I don't think so. I believe they loved each other very much. It is a husband's duty to look after his wife, to ensure her safety at all times."

Sally smiled tightly. "I partially agree. As I said before, Patrick was on duty at the time. He can't be held responsible if an intruder got into the house. Even an alarm wouldn't have helped in that instance." Mrs. Maqsood bowed her head as if she was ashamed of voicing the accusation. "Can you tell me if anyone had any grievances against your daughter, possibly at work perhaps?"

"I don't think so. Not that she confided in me, anyway. Would a work colleague really set out to kill my daughter? I find that impossible to believe. Excuse my ignorance, but in cases such as this, don't you always look at the person closest to the deceased?"

"Again, you're inferring that we should be looking in Patrick's direction."

"Yes, why are you not? Because he's a copper, one of your lot?"

"We have questioned him already and will continue to monitor his behaviour in the coming days, but I have to say that I've been an inspector for six years now, and I didn't pick up anything negative in his reaction to the questions he was confronted with. If anything, I believe your son-in-law is still grieving his wife's passing. Maybe if you'd remained in contact with him over the years, you would have seen that for yourself." Sally bit down on her tongue for snapping at the woman. She noticed Jack turn her way.

Mrs. Maqsood looked aghast at Sally's outburst. "I think you should leave my house now. I will tell my husband of your visit and leave it up to him whether he contacts you or not. I fear the latter after the way you've just spoken to me. Goodbye."

The woman dried her floured hands on a tea towel and marched back up the hallway. Both downcast, Sally and Jack followed her to the front door, where they hurriedly slipped back into their shoes and stepped out of the house. Sally turned, intending to apologise, but Mrs. Maqsood slammed the door in her face.

"Oops... looks like you upset her, boss," Jack said as they walked back to the car.

"You know the one thing I really hate about working with you, Jack?"

He winced and shook his head.

"The fact that you always state the bloody obvious. Get in the car." Sally drove off before Jack had even closed his door.

"No need to have a go at me."

"I wasn't. Do you think she's right?"

"About what? The husband?"

"No, whether she was using the right flat bread recipe—of course what she said about the husband!"

"I don't know. He seemed a decent enough chap to me. It's not like he's jumped into bed with anyone else since his wife's death."

"How do we know? We've only got his word on that."

"Maybe questioning his partner this afternoon will help shed some light on that. Partners tend to share their intimate details when they're on duty."

Sally turned to look at him and then swiftly back at the road as the lights up ahead turned to red. "Are you for real? I don't tell you my intimate details."

"All right, maybe that came out wrong. Not intimate details in that way, but at least I know what's going on in your life. I know you live with your mum and dad and Dex the dog, and I know you're banging the pathologist, Simon."

Sally's mouth opened and closed a few times before she found her voice again. "I'm not *banging* anyone, as you so eloquently put it. Simon and I are dating. There's no law against that as far as I know."

Jack shrugged. "Now don't go getting all defensive on me. I was just stating that I know about your personal life because we chat about these kinds of things."

"Maybe I'll reconsider that in the future. Hey, I hope you haven't spread that around the station? About me and Simon. It's early days."

"Nope, your secret is safe with me, boss. Don't try and pull the wool over my eyes and tell me there's nothing going on, though, especially when you come to work dressed in the same clothes you had on the day before." He pointed ahead of him. "The lights have changed."

Sally seethed. "Too smart for your own good sometimes. Why don't you direct that astuteness to solving the case rather than dissecting my private life?"

Jack burst out laughing as she pulled away from the lights. "You really are in a foul mood today. What's wrong? The doc keep you awake talking about his latest PM, or was he too busy prodding you with his instrument?"

"Jack Blackman! How dare you!" she spluttered, fighting the urge to slap him around the face in case he hit her with an assault charge.

"I dare all right. Only because I know I'm safe while you have your hands on the steering wheel."

"Back to business. It'll be interesting to see what we gather from Hawk this afternoon. As you've adroitly said, it's surprising what partners pick up about each other's personal life." She could feel his smugness but couldn't think what else to say to slap him down. She hated not being able to fire back a smart retort when it was called for.

They stopped off at the local bakers on the way back to the station, and Sally bought sandwiches and cakes for the team to see them through the long afternoon. She hesitated when she ordered Jack's ham and cheese roll, considered asking the assistant to put an extra sprinkling of pepper on it to pay him back for winding her up, but decided against it.

CHAPTER FIVE

Sally ate her lunch while she dealt with the paperwork that had appeared on her desk during her absence. At five minutes to two, she left her office and tapped Jack on the shoulder as she walked through the incident room. "Coming to question Hawk with me?"

"If I have to," he said, rising from his chair.

"No, you don't have to. You stay there. Joanna, want to accompany me?"

The constable leapt out of her seat and snatched up her notebook and pen. "Would love to, boss."

Sally grinned at the gobsmacked expression on Jack's face. "That'll teach you to wind me up, Bullet. Maybe you'll think twice next time. Nice sandwich, was it?"

Jack's nose twitched. "Yeah, it was. Thanks, boss."

"Good. It had something a little extra in there, if you know what I mean."

"You didn't?"

"Didn't what, Jack?" she teased, winking at him. "We'll be back in a while, folks. We'll have a catch-up when I return."

Following Sally out of the incident room, Joanna asked, "Did you, boss?"

"What? Put a little extra in his sandwich? Nah, not this time. Hopefully, it'll make him think before he picks on me again. I love making him squirm like that, ex-soldier or not."

Both of them laughed, but they had straightened their faces by the time they entered Interview Room One.

The redheaded constable sitting at the table turned to look at them when they entered the room.

Sally shook the woman's hand. "Hello, Constable Hawk. All right if I call you Caroline? I'm DI Sally Parker, and this is DC Joanna Tryst."

"Caroline is fine, ma'am."

"Good. Can I just say before we begin that you're not in any trouble? All I want to do is get your take on what happened to PC Thomas's wife. I see from our records that you have been partners with Patrick for the past thirteen years. I know it's asking a lot for you to remember back to the day Aisha lost her life, but if you can try, that'll be a great help."

"Crikey, that is a big ask, ma'am. I'll do my best."

"Primarily, I suppose I'd like to know how Patrick has coped since that awful day occurred?"

"Like anyone else who has grieved a loved one, ma'am. No differently."

"Has he been with anyone else since that day?"

Caroline's gaze drifted down to the table, and she studied her interlocked hands carefully before she replied. After a while, she looked Sally in the eye and shook her head. "Sorry, I was trying to think back over the years, but I have to say no. I don't think he's ever mentioned even being slightly interested in another woman, ma'am, which is a shame. He's a lovely man."

"It is. Grief can be very destructive, especially considering the way Aisha was murdered. Can you think back to the day the incident happened? He found his wife after he'd finished his shift. Is that correct?"

"Yes, ma'am. I got a call late that evening to tell me that she had died. I was devastated for him. No one deserves to come home to a scene like that in their own house."

"Was Patrick pleased how the initial investigation went?"

Caroline contemplated the question then shrugged. "I think so. He just let the guys do their job."

"Even when things ground to a halt, it didn't bother him?"

"Not that I can recall. Are you saying that the officer in charge messed up, ma'am? Is that why the investigation has been reopened?"

"No, I'm not inferring that at all. The case has come to us because some new evidence has presented itself."

Caroline's eyes widened. "Wow, it has? Can I ask what that evidence is, ma'am?"

"No. It's on a need-to-know basis."

"Sorry for asking."

"No need to apologise. I'm sure I would do the same if I were in your shoes. Can I ask if you got involved in the investigation back then?"

"No, ma'am. I was never asked. I suppose because Patrick and I were partners, that would have been frowned upon."

"Maybe you're right. Partner or not, it wouldn't have prevented me from trying to help out."

Caroline frowned. "Maybe if I had inspector epaulettes, it would have been a different story, ma'am, but a PC nosing around would have been seen as interfering with a case."

Sally nodded. "You could have a point there; forget I asked. So, you supported your partner, but tell me, did you ever suspect him?"

Caroline collapsed back in her chair, and her mouth hung open for a second or two. "That's terrible, ma'am. No, I've never thought Patrick would ever have the inclination to do something as horrendous as taking another person's life, let alone killing the woman he was head over heels in love with."

"And were they? In love? Or were they performing some kind of charade for their friends and family? Although, from what we gathered from his mother-in-law, it would appear that some ties had been cut there, am I right?"

"Firstly, yes, Patrick loved Aisha dearly. And secondly, her family suck. They should have supported the marriage. Did her mother tell you that none of Aisha's family showed up for the wedding? Although they did attend the reception afterwards."

"No, that little detail was never passed on to me. Why did they turn up for the reception? Any idea?"

"I'm presuming because the service took place in a church. You know what these people are like?" Caroline said, bitterness evident in her tone.

"'These people'? I'm not understanding where you're coming from, Caroline."

"Sorry, ma'am, I didn't mean that to come across as racist. It's a different culture we're dealing with here. They have rules, or so it would seem, and if those rules are broken, then someone has to pay the price."

Sally couldn't tell if the constable was just being ignorant or if there was another inference entirely behind her words. She leaned forward a little. "Pay the price? Are you suggesting her family might have killed her?"

Caroline shook her head vigorously. "No, ma'am. I merely suggested that she went against her religion, and they punished her by cutting her off."

"And yet they attended the reception. That's very strange."

"It is, ma'am. Maybe that's something you should ask them about."

"I will. Don't worry." Sally's mind was filled with questions, but she didn't want to bombard the constable, so she asked, "Has Patrick ever mentioned if he or Aisha were feuding with anyone at the time of her death?"

"Ma'am? I'm really not understanding this line of questioning. I thought you knew who was responsible for her death: the two burglars. Can't for the life of me remember their names now."

"As I said before, new evidence has come into our possession, and we're just trying to piece the puzzle together."

"Are you dismissing the two burglars, ma'am?"

Sally sighed. "Between you and me, yes."

Caroline fell silent and stared at her hands, twisting on the table. "I can't believe it... after all these years. If there's anything I can do to help, all you have to do is say the word."

"Thank you. All you can do for now is tell us how Patrick has reacted over the years. For instance, has he had bouts of depression? Did he grieve much at the time?"

"I can't really tell you more than I have already. He's always been a quiet, deep-thinking kind of guy. Yes, he suffered from more quiet spells than normal directly after Aisha left us, but that's normal, I would suspect. He's definitely never given me the impression that he was 'in on it'. I told him years ago that he can turn to me if he has a problem that he needs to share. He chooses not to."

"That's sad. Perhaps he has a good family behind him, people he can rely on."

"Both his parents died a few years ago—not long after Aisha, I think—and he was an only child."

Sally puffed out her cheeks. "Okay. Please, can I ask you to keep our meeting to yourself? And if you think of anything more that is likely to help this case, will you ring me?" She pushed a business card across the table.

"Of course. I hope you catch the bastard this time round, ma'am."

"My team and I are going to do our very best to ensure that happens, Caroline."

The three of them stood up and left the interview room together. Caroline marched off ahead of Sally and Joanna.

"What do you make of that?" Sally asked.

"It's all very sad, ma'am. I didn't really gain much from what the constable had to say. Am I missing something?"

Sally turned to smile at her. "I'm not sure. I'll tell you what I think as soon as we get back to the office. I'd like you to look into how Patrick's parents died. Maybe that will point us in a meaningful direction, because at the moment, we really don't have a lot."

"Yes, boss."

They ascended the stairs together. At the top, DCI Green was waiting for Sally. "You go ahead and action what we spoke about, Tryst. I won't be long."

Joanna gave the DCI an awkward smile and trotted away.

"Hello, sir?"

"Inspector. Any news on the cold case yet?"

"Far too early for that, sir. We're working through the list and interviewing anyone involved, but that's going to take time."

"What's your gut instinct telling you on this one?" he asked impatiently.

Sally's mouth turned down, and she shook her head. "Hard to tell at this early stage, sir." *That's all you're getting out of me for now. You can't expect me to come up with the goods after only working on the case for a day. The initial investigating officer worked the case for over six months and failed to come up with the goods.*

He grunted and turned on his heel. "Keep me informed every step of the way, hear me?" he called over his shoulder before he stormed off.

"Yes, sir." She walked towards the incident room with a grin stretching her lips apart. Joanna was looking out for her arrival and motioned for Sally to join her. "What have you found, Joanna?"

"Something or nothing, boss. Depends how you want to look at it. I pulled up the death certificates for Thomas's mother and father. His father died of a heart attack; he suffered from a congenital heart condition for years apparently. That was eight years ago, and the mother died around three months later."

"Of what?"

"Nothing suspicious. She just gave up. Stopped eating and went downhill rapidly. The pathologist said that it was likely that she died of a broken heart."

Sally tutted. "How awful for her, and for Patrick to have to contend with so soon after losing his wife. Not sure how I would have coped under the same circumstances."

"Me neither, if I'm honest, boss. Where do we go from here?"

Sally clapped to draw everyone's attention. "Grab a coffee, folks. Time for a conflab."

Chairs scraped as Jack positioned them in a circle around the incident board. Joanna and Jordan collected the coffees from the machine while Sally contemplated what she was going to say next.

When Joanna handed her a coffee, she took a sip then set the cup down on the desk beside her. Once everyone was settled, she cast her eyes over the team. "The DCI collared me outside to see how the case was progressing. I had to tell him that it isn't—I hate doing that. I know we've only been working on the case less than thirty-six hours, but I need to shift this sinking feeling I have here." She ran her hand across her flat stomach.

"Wish we had more to go on, boss. The truth is we haven't," Jack pointed out unnecessarily.

"So, let's go over what we do have. So far, we've spoken to the victim's husband and mother, and Patrick's partner on the beat. All that has thrown up is that Aisha's parents hated her husband and the fact that they married behind their backs and out of Aisha's faith. Joanna came up with the idea of an honour killing. While I can see why she thought that, I'm not a hundred percent sold on the idea. The mother didn't really come across as being vindictive enough to be involved in that kind of shit, however, we still need to question Aisha's father, get his take on things."

"When do you want to do that?" Jack asked.

"I prefer it if it was either today or tomorrow. The jury is still out for me on Patrick Thomas. He hasn't shown me any reason to suspect he was involved. Conversely, he hasn't really shown why we should discount him, either. According to his partner, he's a quiet man and a deep thinker. He hasn't said anything that could point the finger to him being the culprit over the years. He also had to contend with the loss of both parents a few years after he lost his wife, which would increase any likely grief he might have been suffering from."

"So, what next?" Jordan asked.

"We keep questioning people, beginning with the neighbours. Odds are that they'll have changed since then, but it's something we shouldn't neglect. Plus, we need to visit the school and see what her work colleagues have to say. Jack, you and I will do that. I'd like the rest of you to try and track down anything to do with the burglars—friends, relatives, look into their financial situation if you can find anything after all this time. I want to know why they turned to crime, what sentences they served, if any. You know the drill. Let's keep at it, guys. Something will show up soon. If it doesn't, then we're gonna have the DCI breathing down our necks pretty soon."

"Boss, what about having a word with the leading investigator on the case?" Stuart asked.

"Yep, that's another avenue for Jack and me to pursue. All right, let's drink up and crack on."

CHAPTER SIX

Sally and Jack pulled up outside the semi-detached house that was adjoined to Patrick Thomas's home.

"Not sure I'd be very keen to have this house next to mine. It's a bit of a tip. Don't people care about the value of their homes these days?" Sally grumbled as they walked through the small gate and up the concrete drive. They stood inside the arched porch, knocked on the door, and waited for it to be opened.

Almost a minute passed before a grey-haired gentleman of retirement age greeted them. "Hello? If you're selling double glazing, sling your hook. I ain't interested. Just because my windows need a bit of painting, it don't mean that they don't keep the draft out. Got that?"

Sally smiled. "I'm sorry to disturb you, Mr. Yates. I'm DI Sally Parker, and this is my partner, DS Jack Blackman. Would it be possible to come in and speak to you for a second or two?"

The old man frowned and raised his glasses to look at her properly. "Bloody turning out DIs young nowadays, aren't they? How old are you? Twenty-five?"

Sally felt the colour rushing into her cheeks. "Thirty-one actually, sir. May we come in?"

"Not until you tell me what it's about."

"About an incident that occurred in the neighbourhood ten years ago."

"What? And you're just investigating the case now? I know the police are bloody hopeless these days—didn't realise standards had dropped that much."

In spite of the man's remarks, Sally really liked him, as she could see the similarities to her dearly departed grandfather. "Things haven't got quite that bad yet, sir. We're looking into a cold case."

"Ah, why didn't you say that in the first place? Well, come in out of the cold. Want me to pop the kettle on for you?"

"No, thanks anyway."

Sally and Jack followed him up a grubby hallway and stopped outside the first door on the right. He sat in an upright chair, positioned next to an old oil heater that was throwing out a generous amount of heat considering its age.

"Don't just stand there. Take a seat, the pair of you." The two detectives sat on the sofa opposite him. He laughed when Sally jumped out of her seat again. "Oops, I forgot to tell you to watch out for the killer springs. That needs to go off to the tip, that thing."

Sally turned around and decided to perch on the arm of the chair instead; she noticed Jack was trying hard to suppress a grin. She glared at him, and he averted his eyes back to the old man. "Mr. Yates, am I right in thinking that you've lived at this address for a number of years?"

"That's right. Don't ask me to give you an exact number. I'd say it's probably over twenty years. Why?"

"So you'll remember the incident that happened at number twenty-four, ten years ago?"

"Pretty hard not to remember something like that, duck. Bloody hell, horrendous it was... and to a copper's wife. You just don't expect that kind of shit to go on, not on your own doorstep," he said, shaking his head in disgust.

"It was a sad case. We're revisiting it because we've uncovered vital new evidence—before you ask, I can't really divulge what that evidence is. Can you tell me what you told the investigating officer at the time? Maybe you've thought about something that has bugged you over the years, something you might have left out of your statement?"

"I don't think I left anything out. Pretty sure I told that officer everything I knew."

"Which was?" Sally smiled.

He scratched his temple, and his eyes narrowed as he thought. "Let me see... give me a minute to run through things in my mind. It's a tad rusty after all these years."

"What job did you have, Mr. Yates?"

"I used to be a primary school headmaster."

"How wonderful."

"Hush now, or I won't be able to think properly."

Sally raised her eyebrows at Jack, amused the old man was reprimanding her as if she were one of his students.

Mr. Yates clicked his fingers and nodded. "I remember it all now. It's like a movie replaying in my mind. I was outside letting my cat out—poor thing has gone to pussy heaven now, anyway—and I'd not long arrived home from school when Aisha pulled up. She was always really amiable, had time to speak to people, never cut anyone off, except one person. I'll tell you about him in a second or two."

Sally glanced over at Jack again. "Can't wait to hear that part."

"Anyway, as I was saying, Aisha came home from work and was chatting with me outside. I was wittering on about some student or other excelling at school; it's what teachers do with each other, in case you're interested. The thing is, I could tell she was in a rush, and yet she took time out of her day to stop and talk to me."

"Did she mention why she was in a rush?"

"If I recall rightly, I think she told me that she was going out with a few friends."

"Alone or with her husband?"

"I think she said it was a girls' night out." Mr. Yates suddenly became sad and withdrawn, pulling at a caught thread in his woven trousers. Then he withdrew a linen handkerchief from his trouser pocket and wiped his eyes. Sally felt her own eyes prick—her grandfather had never been without a "proper handkerchief", and it brought the memories of him flooding back. She had cried for a whole week after he'd died, and her heart had been so painful that she'd been forced to go to the doctor for a check-up. The doctor had put it down to her being broken-hearted and said that the grief would subside eventually.

"Are you all right, sir?" she asked quietly, crossing the room. She knelt before him and placed her hand over his.

The man's watery gaze met hers. "I'm all right, dear. I suppose I've only just realised how much I miss the poor girl. She really was one in a million. Which makes it all the more traumatic knowing that I'll never see her again. Oh my, what am I like? She was only a neighbour, for goodness' sake! Anyone would think she was a blood relative. I don't think I've ever felt like this before. Maybe it's a sign I'm getting on in life and becoming an emotional old fool."

Sally patted his hand. "Not at all. It's lovely that you thought so much of her and feel very sad that she died the way she did. Did you notice anyone strange hanging around that day? Hear anything unusual going on in the garden or something like that?"

"No, that was the first thing I tried to think about back then, but I couldn't recall seeing or hearing anything out of the ordinary. Didn't the coppers say that two scumbag burglars killed her?"

Sally nodded, not letting on about the new evidence. "Yes, that's right. What about the days leading up to the incident? Do you remember anything out of the ordinary happening in the street?"

He shook his head.

Jack cleared his throat. "You mentioned something about another neighbour, sir? Can you tell us who you were referring to?" He had his pen poised over his notebook.

Mr. Yates tutted, and his mouth twisted as though he was grinding his teeth. "That bastard Warren Dean. He was always having run-ins with Aisha."

Sally swiftly turned to face Jack, who raised an interested eyebrow as he jotted down the name. "And where did he live?" Sally asked.

"On the other side, at number twenty-six. Nasty piece of goods, he was."

"Does he still live there?" Sally asked.

"No, let me think when he moved out." He clicked his fingers together a second time. "It wasn't long after, if I remember rightly. I had a few choice words to say to him one day. He started mouthing off about Aisha, and I stuck up for her, said that she was worth ten of him."

"When did this confrontation take place? Before or after Aisha's death?"

"It was after as far as I can remember. I didn't hold back, either. I know his type, always fond of bullying women, but when it comes to having an argument with a bloke, they usually back down, bloody cowards."

"So, he confronted her numerous times? Is that what you're telling us, Mr. Yates?"

"Oh, yes. I'd go so far as saying that he used to hang around outside the house waiting for her to come home some days."

Jack looked up from his notebook. "Oh, did he now?"

"Yes. Of course when he saw me, he'd scarper into the house. I used to look out for the lass every night around the time she was due home. She wasn't aware of that, however. Can't abide bloody bullies. I used to deal with enough of them at school, came down heavy on the buggers, too, I can tell you. There's no need for it—we're all equals after all, ain't we?"

Sally nodded. "We are indeed. Thank you for caring about Aisha. Can I ask if Patrick was aware this was going on at the time?"

"I don't think so. Aisha swore me to secrecy; she didn't want 'to bother hubby with her problems' was how she put it. I begged her to let me tell him, but she was adamant. I had to abide by her wishes."

"Daft question coming up: did you tell the original investigating officer about the contretemps Aisha had with this Mr. Dean?"

"I tried to, but he didn't seem interested," he stated, his words full of regret.

"That's sad. Why do you really think Mr. Dean was hounding Aisha, because she was a woman or because of the colour of her skin?"

"Oh, he was a racist, all right. The bigoted exchanges were clear for anyone to hear. Bastard. I was looking out my window one evening, and dusk was rapidly descending, when Aisha came home from work. She parked in the road as usual, and that bastard was out there in his car. I watched him deliberately reverse into her car. She got out of her vehicle shaken up and tried to confront him, but he was vehement and tried to blame Aisha for the accident. I went running out there just as he unleashed a vile racist torrent of abuse. He didn't see me until his horrendous speech had finished. I stood beside Aisha and stuck up for her. I told Dean that I witnessed the supposed accident and that it was no such thing. He mumbled a feeble apology and stormed into his house with his tail between his legs, vile man."

"When did this incident happen? Can you recall?"

"Not long before... you know, she lost her life."

"Do you think he could have been responsible for her death?"

His wide-eyed gaze met Sally's. "He wouldn't have, would he? No, he might have enjoyed shouting his mouth off, but I doubt that he would have had it in him to follow through on any threats he flung at her. I tried to persuade her to tell Patrick; he could've had a word with the weasel or got some kind of restraining order against him, but Aisha pleaded with me not to tell him. She said she'd lived her whole life surrounded by bigots such as Dean, that she was used to seeing the hatred in people's eyes when they confronted her. Why? Why would anyone say a bad word against such a beautiful, vibrant young lady?"

"It's a crazy world we live in, Mr. Yates. It's easy for people to blame a person for the failings of their fellow countrymen. Even though Aisha hadn't lived in Pakistan, persuading people that she had nothing to do with what went on in her country would have been an impossible task. Most people are ignorant about these things. 'Bloody-minded', my old grandmother used to say."

"I fear you may be right, Inspector. To tell you the truth, I can't wait for the time when I have to leave this cruel, twisted bloody world. I never thought those words would come out of my mouth, but there appears to be such a lack of compassion nowadays. Everyone has an angry gene running through them. It never used to be like that when I was a lad. It's heartbreaking and totally disrespectful. Oh dear, sorry, you didn't need to hear me venting like that."

"Nonsense, it's better out than in. It'll only eat away at you, otherwise. Did you ever hear Patrick and Aisha arguing?"

He adamantly shook his head. "No, never. They were a solid couple. I tell you what I did hear through the adjoining wall."

Sally tilted her head. "What was that?"

"A lot of laughter, joyful laughter. They were very much in love, Inspector."

"Then I think our job is done here, Mr. Yates. Unless you can give us a forwarding address for the pleasant Mr. Dean?"

"No, I'm so sorry. I was just pleased to see the back of him when he up and left."

"Did he own the house, or was it rented?"

"Not sure. I believe it might have been rented, only because I never saw a 'for sale' board go up. Can you check that?"

"Yes, we'll get onto the land registry, see what they can tell us." Sally rubbed her hand over his before she stood up. "Are you sure you're going to be okay? We've stirred up some pretty horrendous images for you to have to contend with."

"I'm fine. Thank you for caring. I hope you catch the person responsible."

Sally shook out the pins and needles affecting her legs before she and Jack started to walk back up the hallway and out of the house. Once outside, she turned to face Mr. Yates and extended her hand to give him her card. "I promise you we will solve this case and slam this person in prison. Here are my contact details; feel free to get in touch if you think of anything else or if you ever need a chat."

"You're very kind, Inspector. I'll bear that in mind. Good luck in your quest."

"Thank you."

He gently closed the door behind them. Sally was wracked with emotion as she made her way back to the car with Jack.

"Are you all right, boss?" he asked over the top of the car.

"I'm not sure is the honest answer. As soon as we get back to the station, we need to start looking for Dean. Something just isn't sitting right with me there. He sounds a cold, calculating bastard who certainly had a motive to at least be a person of interest. What do you think?"

"Totally agree. Do you want to hang around here and see what the other neighbours have to say?"

"I know we should, but my gut is telling me to concentrate on this guy, to make tracking him down a priority."

"I hear you. Maybe if the trail goes cold, we can revisit the neighbours. Not sure we should dismiss that altogether just yet, boss."

"You're right. Just go with me on this one for now, Jack. Fancy a pub lunch? My treat. I need to get my emotions in check before we return to base."

"Why not? It's been ages since I tucked into a ploughman's lunch."

After eating their lunch and pulling apart what Mr. Yates had told them, they stopped off to pick up sandwiches for the rest of the team on the way back to the station.

"Interesting development this morning, folks—another possible suspect highlighted by one of the neighbours. Jack is going to try and track down one of the other neighbours who had several run-ins with the victim. We believe the husband was unaware of the problems Aisha had with this man. Nasty piece of work by all accounts. It's something we need to make a start on right away." Sally turned to her right. "What do you have, Joanna?"

"I've been making a list of all Aisha's work colleagues at the time, to see who is still working at the school."

"And?"

"Bit of luck. Looks like everyone is still there, boss."

Sally rubbed her hands together then stuck her thumb up. "I'm getting a good feeling about this now, team. Although the list of suspects is growing, at least we're getting somewhere and not stagnating. Let's try and hit every one of the buggers in the next day or so. Joanna, Jack and I are going out to have a word with Brian Falkirk, the officer who originally dealt with the case."

"We are? We've only just got back—what about tracking the neighbour down?" Jack complained.

"Hand that over to Jordan, if you will. I was thinking it over in the car, and I believe going over to see Falkirk should definitely be our next move.

"Do we have time for a coffee?"

"Yep, I have to make a few quick calls anyway. Be ready for the off in fifteen, okay? Joanna, do me a favour and ring the school, ask the head if it's all right if we drop by and see the teachers after school tomorrow."

"Will do."

"Jordan, I want everything you can find on Warren Dean by the end of tomorrow. Dig deep. Like I said before, he's coming across as a nasty piece of work. I wouldn't put it past him to be the culprit. Something is niggling at my gut about him."

The team got back to work, and Sally stopped at the vending machine to pick up a coffee before continuing to her office. She opened the window as the room felt a little stuffy now that spring had finally sprung. She couldn't wait to get home and take Dex for a walk down by the river. She picked up the phone and dialled home. "Hi, Mum. Just checking in to see if everything is okay."

"I wondered when you were going to ring. We're fine, love. Dex has been sitting by the door, pining for you, as usual. He's too attached to you, that dog."

"Bless him. I'll take him for an extra-long walk when I get home. I was ringing up to say I'll be home around six, as usual. Anything you want me to bring in with me?"

"Not that I can think of, love. Nice of you to grace us with your presence this evening. We'll look forward to that."

"There's no need for sarcasm, Mum. It was only one night away."

"Not sarcasm, dear, more like teasing. Did you have a nice time? I'm not asking you to go into detail, you understand."

Sally smiled and shook her head as she felt the colour rising in her cheeks. "Yes, Simon and I had a lovely meal and catch-up."

"Is there any chance we can meet this young man sometime soon?"

"It's early days yet, Mum. I wouldn't want to scare him off."

Her mother grunted. "Huh! That's charming, I must say."

"Don't go getting shirty with me. You know I didn't mean it like that. I'd rather take things slowly after what happened with Darryl."

"I know, dear. No pressure, I promise. Shall I set an extra place for dinner on Sunday?"

"I thought you said no pressure? Let me have a word with Simon, and I'll let you know tonight. How's that?"

"Very well. I'll nip out to the shops and buy a nice piece of topside just in case. What about a syrup sponge for afters? That should go down a treat."

"And add a couple of inches to my waistline in the process! You're incorrigible. Let me see what Simon has to say first before you start searching for the best recipe." Sally knew what her mother was like—every night until Saturday, she would be frantically turning the pages of her vast selection of recipe books, looking for the best recipes to try, something completely different to the wonderful meals she usually knocked up every day for Sally and her father.

"Okay, dear. I'll see you in a few hours. Your father needs his lunch now."

"See you later." Sally hung up, resting her hand on the phone, tempted to ring Simon to offer the invitation, but something made her hesitate. *I'm being silly. Just because he's asked me to move in with him it doesn't mean that I should treat him any differently.* She relented and dialled his number.

"Hello, Simon Bracknall."

"Hi, it's me. Just wondered how you are." Sally cringed when the words came out. They sounded sappy even to her ear.

"Hello, well, this is an unexpected pleasure. I'm doing well, all things considered. How are you on this wonderfully warm afternoon?"

"Not as chipper as you, obviously. Why the good mood?"

His voice lowered to just above a whisper. "For some reason, I have an extra spring in my step and a lightness in my heart."

"Oh, you do, do you? And why do you think that is?"

"Between you and me, I spent the night with this amazing young lady and even ended up asking her to move in with me."

She breathed a sigh of relief that everything was the same between them, even though he hadn't said goodbye to her before she'd left his house that morning. "Oh, is that right? Well she'd be foolish to turn you down. What did she say?" Sally bit her lip as she waited for his response.

"I think I kind of ruined things a little. Maybe the suggestion came out of the blue and caught her on the hop. Hopefully, she won't think bad of me trying to railroad her into doing something that she wasn't ready to do yet."

"I'm sure she'll come around, if you're patient with her. That's a giant step you've asked her to take."

"I realised that on the drive into work, especially after what she's gone through in the past with her previous partner. I was selfish really. I hope she can forgive me."

"I'm sure things will work out for the best. Just give her time to come around to the idea. Anyway, enough about that. What are you doing on Sunday? Any plans?"

"Hmm... let me think. Nope, no plans as yet. Why?"

"My mum has invited you to dinner. A beef roast and syrup sponge is on the menu if that will help sway your decision." There was a long pause on the line. "Simon? Are you still there?"

"I'm here. Scared shitless at the thought of meeting your folks. How are they going to react to me after knowing what you went through with your ex?"

"Oh no, you mustn't think that. Mum and Dad never judge people like that. You're reading too much into it. Darryl was different."

"He was a charmer with them, wasn't he? What if they think the same way about me, and it raises their suspicions?"

Sally bounced back in her chair, feeling guilty for unburdening herself the way she had. If she hadn't told him about Darryl, he would be feeling less insecure about meeting her parents. She tried hard to undo the damage she had caused. "I'm sorry. I'm at fault here, not you. My parents are fine. They never judge people. They might be a little cautious about meeting you, but surely that's what every parent goes through when they meet their child's boyfriend or girlfriend. Don't you think your parents are going to act the same way if I ever meet them?"

He sighed. "Oops, I suppose you're right. Maybe we can drop in on my parents the following weekend then. How does that sound?"

"Like a challenge to me." She laughed.

"They'll love you as much as I do."

She took the phone away from her ear, stared at it in awe then placed it against her ear again. "You do? You've never told me that."

"Haven't I? I thought it was obvious. You think I make a habit of inviting women to share my home with me?"

"No, not at all. I'm in shock right now. Sorry. Look, I better go. Any news on the burglars' cause of death yet?"

"Ah, the swift change of subject when the conversation becomes too intense. No, I had a traffic accident victim to deal with first thing. I'm just about to start an in-depth PM on them both now."

"Okay, ring me when you find anything out. I'll call you this evening if I don't hear from you before, and Simon…"

"Yes, Inspector Parker?"

"I love you, too." Sally swiftly hung up before he had a chance to answer. Within seconds, a text message jingled on her mobile. She withdrew the phone from her pocket and looked at the message. She found a single red heart filling the tiny screen. Her heart skipped in her chest.

She downed her coffee and left the office with a broad smile stretched across her face and a lightness in her feet. *I deserve to be happy after what Darryl put me through. I just hope nothing happens to mess things up. It all seems too good to be true at the moment.*

Jack eyed her suspiciously. "Are you ready?"

"Yep, I've sourced Brian Falkirk's address. I haven't rung ahead. Did you want me to do that?"

"No, let's shoot over there and take a chance on him being at home."

CHAPTER SEVEN

Sally and Jack leapt out of the car once they arrived at Brian Falkirk's detached bungalow. The cul-de-sac had obviously been built with the retired residents in mind. The rosebed in the centre was just showing signs of buds. Sally thought this road would suit her parents down to the ground. *Stop it. They're happy where they are now that the vile neighbours opposite have been moved on by the council.*

"Nice area," Jack stated as he pushed open the wooden gate to the property.

Sally noticed the smell of freshly mown grass. Clipped grass so early in the year was always a sign of a keen gardener.

Jack did the honours of ringing the bell. Immediately, a tall, grey-haired, bespectacled man opened the door. "You look like coppers to me," he said, frowning.

"You're still very perceptive, Mr. Falkirk. Mind if we come in for a few minutes?" Sally smiled as she showed him her ID.

He leaned closer. "DI Parker, may I ask what this is in connection with?"

"A cold case we've been assigned that you investigated ten years ago."

He nodded, stepping back to allow them in. Sally followed him up the hallway, through the kitchen, and into a glass-walled conservatory.

Jack closed the front door and joined them.

"Care for a cup of tea?"

"I'll get that, dear," Mrs. Falkirk called out from the kitchen, running the tap and filling the kettle.

"Thank you, that would be lovely," Sally called back to the slim, well-dressed lady.

"Take a seat. I presume you're talking about the Aisha Thomas case as that's the only case I left unsolved. It galls me to say that. Every copper wants to have an exemplary arrest record before they retire."

"It is. Actually, some new evidence was discovered this week. That's why my boss has asked us to open it up again."

He frowned and tilted his head. "Don't stop there, Inspector."

"I'd like to leave that part until the end, if you don't mind. I wanted to know what led you to suspect the two burglars were guilty of killing Mrs. Thomas."

"I simply put two and two together. These two—Wilson and Jenkinson, I believe they were called—had been causing havoc in the neighbourhood around that time."

"But had they upped their game and killed anyone?"

"Not that I recall. You know how it is, Inspector. Criminals get used to the buzz of outwitting the police, and it's not uncommon for these guys to change their MO on occasion."

"Did they leave any evidence at the scene, for you to put them in the frame?"

He fell silent as he thought back. Then he shook his head. "No, I can't say they did."

"Then I have to say I'm a little disappointed and flummoxed as to why you would offer them up as the prime suspects. Why was that?"

Falkirk fidgeted in his seat as Mrs. Falkirk entered the conservatory and placed a tray of mugs and a plate of biscuits on the wicker table in the middle of the room between the two wicker sofas occupied by Sally, Jack, and Brian Falkirk. She smiled and left the room again.

Falkirk waited for his wife to leave the room then closed the door. He returned to his seat. "It was all we had at the time."

"Really? Because these two men were robbing the neighbourhood, you thought they'd be capable of, and wouldn't think twice about, killing a copper's wife?" Sally asked, her voice strained with disbelief.

"It's what we had. There was another murder around that time, I believe."

Sally raised an enquiring eyebrow at Jack, who shrugged and continued to take notes. "Go on. This didn't appear in the case files, or if it did, I must have missed it."

"An old woman—bedridden, she was. I forget the name. I think she lived a couple of streets away from the Thomas house. Again, I had no evidence at that address but wrapped that case up early by pointing the finger at the burglars."

"And you don't think that was a little naïve of you?"

"Not in the slightest. It was a good residential area, and crimes were being committed around the same time, so I pieced all the pieces together and..."

"Came up with an implausible solution. And your commanding officer at the time didn't pull you up on it?"

"I don't know what you're trying to insinuate here, but I'm sure you'd do the same thing in my shoes."

Sally vehemently shook her head. "You're wrong. I wouldn't assume anything until there was evidence to back up my theory, but you had none. This old lady, was there anything reported missing from her home?"

"I had no way of knowing. She was dead when we got there. According to the neighbours, she had no living relatives we could contact, hence the reason the trail went cold pretty damn quick."

"I can't believe what I'm hearing. Was her handbag at the scene?"

"I seem to recall it was."

Sally sucked in a large impatient breath. "And was her purse inside?"

He reached for his mug of tea, took a sip then nodded. "Yes, I think so."

"And you still attributed her death to a burglary? Isn't that the first thing a burglar would take?"

He replaced his mug on the table, sat back in his chair, and glared at her. "All right, maybe I screwed up on that one, dismissed her death too quickly..."

"You reckon? Why? Because she was old and bedridden and didn't have a family?"

"Maybe. Don't tell me you've never done the same in your time on the force."

Sally laughed, flabbergasted by the man's obvious lack of principles. "Are you for bloody real? Of course I've never done that. Have you, Jack?"

Jack's gaze rippled between Sally and Falkirk and finally settled back on his partner. "Umm... never been tempted to do that, either, boss. You'd yank my balls off and shove them in my mouth if I even suggested such a thing."

Sally smiled despite her anger. "You're right, I would." She turned to face Falkirk and said, "And your DCI should have done the same. I'm disappointed that you dismissed this woman's death so swiftly. Every victim deserves their case to be investigated thoroughly."

Falkirk's chin dipped to his chest. He seemed ashamed by her reprimand, but perhaps he was just feeling sorry for himself. "I'm sorry. I can see now that my actions were wrong."

"Okay, we'll let that one slip... for now. This morning, we visited the victim's neighbour, a Mr. Yates. He used to be a headmaster. Do you recall interviewing him at the time of Aisha's death?"

He scratched his head. "I think so. Why? What's he said that I did wrong?"

"Please, I'm not on some kind of witch hunt here. I'm simply trying to figure out who killed a serving police officer's wife. Bear with me."

Falkirk nodded.

"Mr. Yates mentioned another neighbour he had concerns about, a Mr. Warren Dean. Can you remember that conversation?"

He shrugged. "I recognise the name. Couldn't tell you in what context, however."

"He said that he highlighted the fact that Warren Dean appeared to have some sort of vendetta against Aisha Thomas, but that you didn't seem bothered about the information. Can you tell me why?"

"Because by then I had my suspects in mind."

"And that's it? Is that how you solved all your cases? Once you had a suspect in mind, there was no deterring you from throwing the book at that suspect?"

He ran a hand through his short hair and bit his bottom lip. "Yes. Please don't tell me that you spend your time looking for suspects when you have identified a probable suspect already?"

"Too bloody right, especially when there is no damn evidence to back up that speculation. For your information, Mr. Yates informed us that Warren Dean used to wait for Aisha to come home and start harassing her before she even stepped in the house. To me, that behaviour would flag him up as a definite suspect."

"I didn't know."

"No, because you were fixated with the two burglars, or was it because you wanted an easy life?"

"Easy life? Are you kidding me? No copper has an easy life."

"I have to be honest with you. That is not why I signed up to the force. I joined to chase down the criminals and to rid our streets of people keen to bring pain and hardship to the general public."

"Yeah, me, too," Falkirk mumbled, his eyes narrowing as he stared at her.

Sally sighed. She hadn't finished with this jerk yet. She intended to make him squirm a lot more. "During your investigation, did you ever interview the husband?"

"I don't understand."

"As a suspect?" Jack asked harshly.

Sally could tell that her partner's patience was running out almost as fast as her own. "Yes, as a suspect," she added.

"No. Why? I didn't see any reason to."

Sally clicked her fingers together. "That's right, because as far as you were concerned, the burglars were the culprits, and no one else was in the frame, right?"

"For the thousandth time—yes, that's right."

"What about Aisha's parents? Did you ever question them?"

"About killing their own daughter? Now you're being downright ridiculous. I'm not sure what kind of police training they issued you with, love, but to think the parents had a hand in this is just so far off the mark it would be regarded as lunacy."

"Really? Jack, would you like to enlighten the gentleman why we believe the parents might be suspects?"

Jack looked up from his notebook and said two words: "Honour killing."

"What? No way. Not in a million years in this country."

"I see you don't keep up with the news on TV then?"

"Nope, most of it is made-up crap. Now I'm confused. So, who are you saying killed their daughter?"

"That's just it. We've only been on the case for a few days, and already, the suspect list is growing. How long did you work on the case? Six months or so?"

"Yeah, but... it was the burglars," he repeated with a defiant glare.

Sally shook her head. "You're sooo wrong about that. Going back to Patrick, did you interview his partner, Caroline Hawk, as to what his state of mind was at the time?"

"No, there was no need. I could see for myself the man was bereft. Hang on, you keep coming back to Patrick. Are you telling me that you have him as your main suspect?"

"I'm not saying that in the slightest, however, you know how many of these types of cases point to the husband killing the wife. We can't discount him, especially with the new evidence we've uncovered."

"You mentioned that when you arrived, and yet you haven't told me what that evidence is."

"Now I've pointed out where you went wrong, I'll tell you. The culprits couldn't have been Wilson and Jenkinson because their bodies—or should I say skeletal remains—have recently been discovered."

"What?" Falkirk shouted, his eyes as bulbous as snooker balls.

"That's right. It looks like they were both killed around the same time and buried close to Thetford Forest."

"That's too bizarre for words."

"Here's another fact you should be interested in: the pathologist tried to match the bite mark on Aisha's arm to the two corpses, but it proved to be a negative result. Therefore, they are completely exonerated, at least in my book. Hence the reason behind our visit today and why my DCI has ordered a full review of the case. Did you even bother to match either of the men's dental records to the bite mark on Aisha's arm?"

Falkirk's head dropped again, and he mumbled, "I screwed up, didn't I?"

Sally couldn't believe it when a lump formed in her throat, and she actually felt sorry for the former inspector. "Let's put it this way. I think you're guilty of taking your eye off the ball. We're looking at this case with fresh eyes and the benefit of hard evidence, something that you and your team never had at your disposal back then. However, I don't care whose toes I step on. I will find Aisha's killer and the person who killed Wilson and Jenkinson, too. Whether the crimes are connected, we'll just have to wait and see. I'm not sure if you're still in contact with anyone at the station or not, but I'm asking you to keep this meeting confidential. Can you do that for me?"

He nodded. "Of course. I can't apologise enough for messing up the way I did. I hope you catch the perpetrator or perpetrators. My door is open if you need any more assistance on the case."

Sally rose from her chair, leaving her cup of tea untouched, while Jack swiftly downed his drink before he followed her back through the house. She smiled at Mrs. Falkirk, who was standing in the kitchen, preparing vegetables for the couple's evening meal.

Falkirk seemed a little awkward as he held open the door. "Thanks for agreeing to see us today, Mr. Falkirk."

"Anytime. Sorry I couldn't be much help in the end."

Sally and Jack waved farewell.

"What did you make of that?" Sally asked after they jumped into the car.

Jack shook his head. "Maybe that's how they did things back then."

"No way. Jack, we're talking ten years ago, not blooming fifty. I'm going to have to take this to the DCI. I dread to think what the repercussions are going to be or how many innocent people are sitting in prison right now because of that man's inept policing skills."

"Whoa, seriously?"

Sally started the engine and nodded. "I'm dead serious about this. I can't frigging believe what I just heard back there. You can't tell me this case is a one-off, not after listening to his explanation of why he thought the burglars committed the crime and why he refused to point the finger elsewhere. What a bloody cock-up!" Sally put the car into gear and pulled away from the kerb.

"Do you think that's why he looked so upset at times? Because he realised the likelihood of you reporting him?"

"I reckon so. That was all about him, not the victims or the innocent people he's banged up. My bet is that he's fearing his pension could be stripped from him."

"Wow! I never even thought of that aspect. Do you really want to do that to him, boss?"

Sally slammed on the brakes and stared at her partner open-mouthed for a second or two. "I can't believe you just said that, Jack. Don't make me out to be the evil bugger in all this." Sally crunched into first gear and pulled off again, seething that her partner should think that way. The rest of the journey was spent in silence.

When they arrived at the station, she told Jack to go back to the incident room while she went in the opposite direction to see DCI Green. She knocked on his door, heard him talking on the phone, and waited for him to invite her in. Minutes later, the call came. Sally walked into the room, and he seemed surprised to see her.

"Inspector Parker?"

"I think we need a chat, sir. All right if I sit down?"

"This sounds ominous. Is it to do with the cold case?"

"In a way, sir." Sally proceeded to recount her conversation with Brian Falkirk.

DCI Green sat back in his chair, constantly tutting and shaking his head as he listened to what she had to say. "That's incredible. It's like listening to a case dating back to the days of Jack the Ripper."

"That's not all, sir. I believe that if Falkirk was capable of this kind of stupidity once, then who's to say he didn't treat the other investigations he was tasked with the same way?"

DCI Green bounced forward in his chair and placed his hands on the desk. "What? You think that's possible?"

"Don't you, sir? We can't dismiss my theory. What if I'm right? What if dozens of innocent men have been imprisoned by this imbecile? He was an inspector for fifteen years, sir. I'm not one to stir up trouble, but it galls me to think what might be at stake here."

"He might be guilty of being a prick on this one case, Inspector, however, we'd be treading on dangerous ground if we start shouting the odds about the other cases he's overseen. CPS wouldn't have let it happen, would they?"

"I have no idea of knowing that, sir."

"Bloody hell! What if he worked over a hundred cases during his career? If we go with your theory, every single one of those cases would need to be reopened and reinvestigated from scratch. Can you imagine the cost implications in that?"

"Are you suggesting we simply ignore this, sir?" Sally asked, dumbfounded by the way the conversation was heading.

"I'm saying that I should think this dilemma over for a while before making our concerns public. Maybe I'll delve into a couple of the cases he solved on the quiet. Yes, that's what I'll do. Leave this with me. I'm trusting you to stay schtum about this, Inspector."

"Why, sir? Because a retired inspector's pension could be in jeopardy if word gets out?"

"Not just because of that, but it's a start, yes. Think of all the inmates' families involved in this. If word reaches the press... well, it doesn't bear thinking about."

Sally stood up and made her way to the door, her stomach churning and tying itself in knots. The last thing she wanted was to be involved in a corrupt police force. Once the press got hold of the truth, every officer at the station would be scrutinised. "I'll leave it with you, sir," she said from the doorway.

"You do that. I'll be in touch when I have anything to share on the matter. Until then, discretion is the keyword."

Sally shook her head all the way back to the incident room, ashamed at what a fellow officer was capable of and frustrated that the DCI was willing to shove this under the carpet if the few cases he studied turned out to be okay in his book.

Joanna looked up at her when Sally entered the room. "I rang the school, boss. Everything has been set up for you for tomorrow at four p.m."

"Excellent news, thanks." She glanced at the clock on the wall. Five fifteen. "Right, I know it's a little early, but I've had enough for one day. I'm off home. Finish up what you're doing and skedaddle, too, all right?"

Jordan gave her the thumbs-up while the rest of the team nodded. Sally collected her bag and coat from the office then headed to the car park. Jack caught up with her as she was about to open the driver's door to her car. She raised a hand to prevent him from speaking. "Don't start, Jack. I've had all I can stand for one day."

"What's up, Sally? This isn't like you. You never leave work early."

She shrugged as unexpected tears moistened her eyes. "Maybe that's where I've been going wrong all these years. Maybe I should start taking the piss around here like other inspectors do, and have done, over the years."

He leaned against the side panel of her car and folded his arms. "I take it things didn't go too well with Green?"

"You take it right. Honestly, Jack, I really don't think I'm cut out for this job anymore. I bust a gut daily to do things by the book, but am I the only one?"

"Don't tar me—or the rest of the team—with the same brush as Falkirk, Sally."

"I'm not. Don't twist my words. I'm talking about other inspectors on the force, love. What's the point in being a good guy? How many more corrupt officers are we going to come across?"

"I think you're being a tad harsh. This is one case he's screwed up. Let's not get things out of proportion here. What did Green say about the other cases?"

"He said he was going to have a discreet look at them to see if he can spot any doubt to the sentences. I can imagine that will only take him an hour or two to complete. He isn't going to look in depth into this, not the way we are with this case. Am I wrong to think that, Jack?"

"I hear you." He shrugged. "What's the alternative?"

Sally looked around the car park before she answered. "That's just it! I haven't got a damn clue. If he says everything shapes up perfectly, I'm going to go through the rest of my life with huge doubts reverberating around my head. Maybe I should ring Lorne, see what she makes of all this. She's used to dealing with more crap along these lines than I am. That's it—that's what I'll do. I'll take Dex for a long walk by the river then ring my old mate. She'll give me the guidance I need."

"Sorry I couldn't be more help, boss. Never come across anything like this before either on the force or in the army."

She rubbed his upper arm. "Don't blame yourself, Jack. It's a tough situation, one that needs careful consideration before any action is taken. Go home, give Donna and the kids a hug from me. I'll see you bright and early in the morning."

"Will do. Drive safely. I'm sure everything will turn out okay."

"I hope so, Jack. If it doesn't, I won't think twice about handing in my notice."

Jack stepped away from the car, a look of shock on his face.

CHAPTER EIGHT

At home, a super-excited Dex greeted Sally, wagging his tail and screeching in a high-pitched whine. She got down on her knees to cuddle her fur baby, whom she had missed dearly. His golden hairs clung to her black suit instantly as if it were Velcro.

"Just look at the state of you now, Sally." Her mother laughed from the end of the hallway.

"I don't mind, Mum. I'll just nip upstairs and get changed into my jogging suit and take him out for a long walk before dinner, if that's all right?"

"Of course it is. Any reason why you're home early? Everything okay down at the station?"

"Yeah, I'll tell you about it over dinner. No need to screw your nose up. It's not a gruesome tale—well, that's not quite true, but I promise to leave out the bloody bits."

"Phew, that's a relief. Steak-and-kidney pie for dinner. It'll be ready in an hour. Does that give you enough time to take the boy out for a long walk?"

"Perfect, thanks, Mum. You're a treasure." She patted Dex on the head then pecked her mum on the cheek before running up the stairs two at a time to get changed. Dex bounded up beside her. Within a couple of minutes, she was togged up in her purple jogging suit and descended the stairs again to put on her trainers. She placed her mobile phone in her pocket with Dex bouncing around at her feet, anxious for his leash to be attached. "Stand still, Jumping Bean. We'll get out a lot faster if you do."

They set off at a brisk pace towards the river, which was at least a ten-minute walk from the house. The evening sun warmed her face, and she sucked in a few large lungfuls of fresh, clean air along the way. Dex trotted along beside her, cocking his head now and again. All seemed well in her life until she summarised what had happened at work during the course of the day. When she reached the river bank, she unhooked Dex from his leash and let him wander freely. He never ventured very far. Sally withdrew her phone and pressed the speed dial for Lorne Warner, who answered almost immediately.

"Hello, stranger. I was going to try and find time to catch up with you this weekend. Well, have you done the deed with that handsome pathologist yet?"

"Lorne Warner, is that all you think about?"

"I wish. Most of the time I have a dozen cases roaming around in my head. Okay, that might be a slight exaggeration on my part, but you get my drift. And you haven't answered my question."

"Yes."

"What? That's amazing. Do I have to add a new wedding hat to my shopping list this weekend?"

Sally laughed. "Bloody hell, woman, give us a chance to see if we like each other or not first."

"You obviously like each other, or you wouldn't have done the *deed*. I'm so pleased for you, hon."

"As it happens, Simon did in a roundabout kind of way invite me to move in with him this morning."

"Bloody hell, he doesn't hang around, does he?"

"My thoughts entirely, which is why I turned him down."

"Damn! I hope you said it tactfully."

"Of course I did. What do you take me for? I think he loves me as much as I love him, but..."

"But what? That's all that matters, isn't it? Hey, time's passing you by swiftly, hon, if you want to start a family."

"Whoa! Who said anything about starting a family? That's the last thing on my mind, especially when I see the state Jack turns up in every morning after a sleepless night with his granddaughter."

"You forget about things like that, eventually," Lorne assured her.

"Nope, not the slightest bit interested. Simon is coming over on Sunday to meet Mum and Dad, and that should be interesting. Dad's bound to give him a grilling."

"They'll get on great. Stop worrying about it."

"This isn't just a personal call. I'm in a bit of a dilemma and need your expert advice about something, if that's okay?"

"All right, let me sit down a sec. Fire away."

Cold Case

Sally sighed, her eyes constantly on her four-legged friend as she continued her walk. "Well, I've been given a cold case to investigate, but something has come to light that doesn't sit comfortably with me. I just wondered how you would deal with the situation if it ever arose on your patch."

"You've definitely caught my interest. Go on."

"Well, this cold case has come up because the corpses of two criminals the investigating officer pinned a murder on suddenly got unearthed the other day. The pathologist—sorry, Simon seems to think that these two men died around the same time as the victim they were suspected of killing."

"Okay, I'm with you so far. What's the problem?"

"After questioning only half the people who were initially involved in the case, I've already flagged up *several* possible suspects, none of whom the SIO at the time even considered. He just presumed known burglars in the surrounding area committed the crime."

"Bloody hell, that's outrageous. Have you discussed the matter with the investigating officer?"

"Yeah, Jack and I went to see him this afternoon, and he more or less said that once he set his eye on a suspect, nothing swayed his decision."

"What? What about the evidence?"

"That's just it—there wasn't any at the time."

"So how was he able to pin the crimes on these two men?"

"Because of their activities as burglars. I know, I know, absolutely bizarre."

"Too blooming right. So, what's happened for you to think these men aren't connected to the crime?"

"The victim had a bite mark on her arm. When Simon discovered the bodies of the burglars, the first thing he did was try to match the bite to either of the two corpses. Neither of them matched."

"Holy crap, and this SIO didn't bother to try and match that bite mark to anyone else at the time?"

"No. The husband is a serving police officer."

"Bloody hell, this just gets better and better. Are you saying he also discounted the husband from his enquiries?"

"Virtually straight away. Plus the parents."

"Why would the parents have killed her?"

"One of my team highlighted that the victim was Muslim and possibly that an honour killing might be on the cards. I've spoken to the mother, and she seemed innocent enough, but who can tell these days. I've yet to question the father."

"Well, you're right to think along those lines. We've dealt with a few similar cases over the years. Not pleasant at all, I can tell you."

"I'm going off track a little here. I've also got a possible racist as a neighbour who used to verbally abuse the victim on a daily basis, according to another neighbour who tried to tell the SIO, but he was having none of it. My dilemma is that I'm wondering how many other cases the inspector has treated in this way. The cold case was his only unsolved case, by the way."

"Hmm... that is a huge dilemma. Have you spoken to your DCI about this?"

"Yeah, fat lot of good that was. He said he's going to *peruse* a couple of his cases, see if they worked out okay."

"The only saving grace in all this is that the Crown Prosecution Service have strict guidelines to adhere to. Still, it's not uncommon for a bent copper to plant evidence here and there in order for a charge to stick. I'm not saying that's happened with this guy, but who knows?"

"You can see why this is such a quandary for me. Here's the toughie: can I ask how you would handle the situation? I'm sure this kind of thing would be more likely to occur in your neck of the woods than mine usually."

Lorne tutted. "I suppose every force in the UK comes across a bent copper now and again, but can't say I've had to deal with any personally, thank goodness. If anything like this did show up on my patch, I'd pull the officer in question into the station for a strict Q&A session. Watch his reaction and go from there. Make sure everything is taped and filmed so you have something to back you up if things get nasty."

"This guy is retired now. Could I still go after him?"

"Most definitely. The force won't want to be forking out a pension on someone they can prove is bent."

"Should I leave things as they are until the DCI comes back with his findings? I've got several other people to interview concerning the cold case, and I'm on a time limit to solve that one."

"I would try and conclude the case and revisit the parts that don't sit comfortably with me afterwards. That would include anything to do with this former investigating officer. Look, you know where I am if you need any advice, hon."

"Thanks, Lorne, you're the best pal a girl could have. No bullshit, either."

"Likewise. Ring me, okay?"

"Enjoy your evening. Oops... Dex has wandered off. I better go and find him. Speak soon." Sally disconnected the call and shouted, "Dex, here, boy." There was no response. "Dex, do you want some dinner? Chicken! Sausage!" She called out, her voice sounding more panicked, and her stomach churned into knots as she mentioned the two favourite foods that always made his ears prick up.

Sally ran along the edge of the water to see if he'd fallen in. Although he was a Labrador, he rarely ventured into the water. "Jesus, Dex, where are you?" She spun around on the spot, carefully examining the area in all directions. She couldn't see his golden coat highlighted by the evening sun anywhere. She started running, calling his name. Still nothing. Tears began to form in her eyes and trickle down her cheeks as she jogged up and down.

Another walker appeared around the bend with a beagle on his extended lead. "Please, have you seen my dog? A golden lab," she asked breathlessly.

The middle-aged man shook his head. "Sorry, love, no. Would you like me to help you look for him?"

"That would be so kind of you. He's never run off like this before. I was distracted making a call, and he just disappeared."

"No problem, we're in no rush to get home. What's your dog's name?"

"Dexter, but he always comes to Dex."

"I'll look this way," the man said. "We'll reconvene back here in five minutes. How's that?"

Sally smiled and placed her hand on his arm. "I can't thank you enough for this."

"I'm sure you'd do the same, love."

Sally agreed. "I would indeed." She turned and hurried along the bank again, searching behind the small trees and shrubs close to the river bank, but found nothing. Dark thoughts entered her mind, mostly statistics of the dog-nappings that were blighting the UK. *Don't think that way. He's here somewhere—he has to be.* She pulled her phone out of her pocket and rang home. "Dad, can you come and help me look for Dex? I'm in the usual place down by the river. I'm scared, Dad. He never runs off."

"On my way, love. I'll bring the car. It'll be quicker."

Suddenly, she heard a distant noise. Unsure what it was, she tilted her head to see if she could hear it again. There—a slight whimper. "Dex... Dex, where are you? I'm here, boy. Keep talking to me. Mummy's here, baby." Hearing another whimper, Sally headed in its direction. She came to a large clump of shrubs, and the whimpering intensified. She pushed aside a thick shrub and gasped. Dex was lying beneath the shrubs, his four legs bound together with rope and silver duct tape wrapped around his muzzle.

Dropping to her knees next to Dex, Sally screamed out to the man who was helping her. "I've found him. He's over here."

The man set off at a gallop and doubled back to be with her. Within seconds, he was standing beside her, staring down at the whimpering Dex. "My God, who'd do such a thing?"

"I don't know. Have you got a penknife on you?"

"Yes, attached to my keyring. Please, let me do it. Your hands are shaking too much. You might cut him."

Sally nodded, stroking Dex's head, trying to comfort her petrified companion with soothing words, while the man cut away the rope from his legs. Dex tried to sit upright, but Sally forced him back down so the man could snip through the tape around his nose. Dex struggled and whimpered as the blade got near his face.

"It's all right, boy. I won't hurt you, not intentionally anyway," the man said, trying to placate Sally's beloved pet.

"Stay strong, boy." Sally's heart was racing like an express train. She found it hard to breathe.

The man sliced through the tape and ripped it off Dex's face. Her dog yelped in pain, jumped to his feet and snarled at the man. Sally stood up and got between the man and Dex. "It's all right, boy. The man was trying to help us." Sally touched the bare patch of skin on the top of his nose where the glue had ripped off his fur.

"He'll be fine. Might not trust any strangers for a while, but there's no lasting damage done to his body anyway."

"Sally, where are you?"

She turned to see her dad racing along the river bank towards them. "Over here, Dad. We've found him."

The man reached out, looked her in the eye, and said, "Take care of Dex."

"I will. I can't thank you enough for what you've done."

The man nodded and walked away in the opposite direction to her father. When her dad was close enough, she fell into his arms and sobbed.

"There, there, love, Dex is safe. What's this all about?"

Sally pushed away from her father's chest. Her hand dropped down to her side and patted Dex's head. "It was awful, Dad. Someone bound his legs up and put tape around his mouth." She pointed to the remnants of the items lying on the ground next to Dex.

"What? That's crazy. Why would anyone do such a horrid thing?"

"I don't know. That man helped me. Not sure I could have removed that tape from Dex's mouth myself. He didn't react very well when it was ripped off."

"I'm not surprised—that stuff hurts. Come on, let's get you and baldy home."

On the ride back to the house, Sally sat in the backseat of the car and hugged Dex all the way. She was guilt-ridden for being distracted by work business instead of keeping a proper eye on him.

Her mother was just as pleased to see Dex as he was to see her. He trotted into the kitchen in search of his evening meal. "Thank goodness you found him," her mother said, wiping her hands down the front of her apron and stroking Dex.

Sally burst into tears again and sobbed as she collapsed into the chair behind her. "Mum, it was awful."

Her father then explained what had happened, anger prominent in his tone. "I hope it wasn't that lot we got evicted from over the road to blame for this."

Sally stared at him. "No, not after all this time, Dad, surely."

Her mother crossed the room and wrapped her arm around Sally's shoulder. "It doesn't matter now. He's safe, and that's the important thing."

Despite their meal tasting delicious, none of them had much of an appetite. The same couldn't be said for Dex. He gobbled his meal then came to sit at the table, waiting for the remains of theirs. Sally cleared the table and started on the washing up. Halfway through the chore, her mobile rang.

"You take that, love. I'll finish this off," her father said, smiling and pushing her aside.

Sally answered the phone on the way into the lounge, and Dex sat on the sofa next to her. "Hi, I was going to ring you later."

"You sound down. Is everything okay?" Simon asked.

"A bit of a mishap when I took Dex out for his evening walk."

"Did he pull you over?"

"No, someone dog-napped him and tied him up."

"What? Are you winding me up?"

"I would never joke about something like that, Simon. I've been in bits since I came home."

"Sorry, you should have rung me."

"I was preoccupied searching for my dog," she snapped uncharacteristically. "Sorry, you didn't deserve that. Ignore me. I was scared. He's fine now. What are you ringing for?"

"Can't I call to see how you're doing?"

"We saw each other this morning, and I rang you at work during the day." *I shouldn't be taking my bad mood out on him.*

"Okay, I'll leave the business talk until tomorrow then. I apologise for disturbing you at home. Glad Dex is safe and well."

"Simon, don't go. I'm sorry. I didn't mean to shut you out. It was horrendous." Tears cascaded down her cheeks again as she recalled the image of Dex trussed up in the undergrowth.

"Look, I'm just about finished here. Do you want me to drop by?"

"No, honestly, I'm fine. All I want to do is cuddle one man tonight—that's Dex. I just feel so damn guilty."

"Why? What have you got to feel sorry about?"

"If I hadn't rung Lorne, I could have kept a proper eye on him."

"These things happen, love. There's no need to blame yourself. Did you catch the bastard who did it?"

"No, there was no one around, except the man who was helping me look for Dex. Do you think someone targeted Dex? Do people usually carry around duct tape and string with them?"

"Not in my experience. Maybe Dex wasn't targeted as such. Perhaps he was in the wrong place at the wrong time. Have you taken him to the vet?"

"No, he seems fine. He wasn't tied up for long, ten minutes at the most. I'll keep an eye on him. He's eaten his dinner. If there was anything wrong, he would be off his food. Enough doom and gloom—how are Wilson and Jenkinson's PMs going? Have you managed to find the COD yet?"

"Not conclusive, however, I found several nicks on the hyoid bones on each victim. Possible or probable cause for that is having their throats cut, the same as Aisha."

"Which probably indicates that we're searching for the same culprit, yes?"

"I'd go along with that theory. I'll keep searching, see if I can find anything else, but I just wanted you to hear what we had so far."

"Thanks, Simon. Sorry for snapping at you earlier."

"No problem. I can't wait to meet the other man in your life on Sunday."

"Glad my abysmal behaviour hasn't put you off. Mum and Dad are really looking forward to meeting you."

"You were stressed. It's understandable. There's nothing to forgive. I'll let you get some rest then, probably speak to you tomorrow."

"Thanks for ringing, Simon. Have a good evening."

Her mother coughed from the doorway. "Didn't mean to eavesdrop, dear. Would you like a coffee?"

"No problem, Mum. It was Simon. He's keen to meet you on Sunday. A coffee would be lovely, thank you."

"You stay there. We'll be in shortly. I'm looking forward to Sunday and meeting the man who has captured your heart, too. It's wonderful to see a smile on your face again."

"I wasn't aware that I was smiling," she replied, her cheeks burning.

Her mother left the room, and Sally pulled Dex tighter to her and kissed his nose. "How are you, my handsome boy?"

Dex licked the side of her face and rested his head against her chest. All was right in his world again, and it was beginning to take shape in hers again, finally.

CHAPTER NINE

The rain was lashing down when Sally pulled into the station car park the next day. She protected her head with her coat and ran for cover. Jack was waiting by the entrance, under the entrance porch, for her to join him.

"Nice day, if you have gills," he joked. When Sally didn't crack a smile, he asked, "Everything all right?"

"Yeah, I'll fill you in later. How are things at home?"

"The usual. I'm here if you need a chat."

Sally rubbed his arm. "Thanks. We need to crack on with the case ASAP this morning."

They rushed up the stairs to the incident room to find the rest of her team already at their desks, working. "Morning, all. Any news come in overnight?"

The other three members of the team shook their heads.

"Okay, I received a snippet of news last night from the pathologist. He believes all three victims were killed by the same person. So, if we find the killer for Aisha, we can bang them up on all three charges."

"All we need to find now is a connection between the three victims," Jack said.

"Exactly. We're going to need to question every family member we can find during the day, not forgetting that Jack and I have an appointment with the teachers at the school this afternoon at four. Any news on Warren Dean yet?"

Joanna shook her head. "Yes and no, boss. I've managed to track down what haulage firm he works for. The bad news is he's been working abroad, filling in for a driver in Germany, for the last month or so."

"Any idea when he's due to return to the UK?"

"They couldn't tell me that, said they would contact me as soon as he docks."

Sally raised a questioning eyebrow. "Can you really see that happening?"

Joanna shrugged. "We'll have to wait and see, boss. I'm still delving into his background. He's got a record. Was banged up on a GBH charge for eighteen months. I've located his address, not far from where he used to live."

"Excellent work. Do me a favour and contact Border Control, put him on the person-of-interest list. That way, we won't have to rely on his firm contacting us when he lands on our shores again."

Joanna turned to face her desk. "I'll get on it now, boss."

Sally stopped at the coffee machine on her way into the office. She opened the window, which was steamed up because of the rain, then settled behind her desk.

Jack entered the room moments later. "Any decision on what we're going to do about what Falkirk said yesterday?"

She waved her hand in front of her. "I've left it with the DCI. I called Lorne last night to get her take on things, and she said it's not unheard of for coppers to falsify evidence."

"Maybe down there and in the larger forces, it's a done thing, but we ain't used to that kind of shit around here. Bit of a shocker to unfold, that was."

"Having slept on it, I have to say I think we've got enough on our plate to deal with right now, Jack. Let's see what Green does about it. If he's got any balls, he'll make sure Falkirk's cases are reinvestigated. Personally, I can't see it working out that way. All I can say is my conscience is clear. I passed the information to my superior officer to take action."

He tapped the side of his nose and pointed at her. "I'm with you. I think if I were in your shoes, I'd pass the buck in the DCI's direction, too. Smart move."

She rubbed her chest. "It still hurts the heart, Jack. What if there are dozens of innocent people sitting in prison because of a bent copper?"

"I know. Let's hope you're wrong about that. Anything specific you want me to tackle?"

"Just make sure we have all the information we need ready for the school visit this afternoon. Do some background checks, see if anything comes up. Also, get a list of family members we need to visit regarding Wilson and Jenkinson. Maybe we can squeeze some of those in this afternoon, before we're due at the school. I need to spend some time in the office today before this paperwork gets out of hand."

He smiled. "I can take a hint. I'll leave you to it."

Alone again, Sally wasn't in the mood for tackling the boring paperwork, so she picked up the phone on the desk. "Hi, it's only me. How are you?"

"Hello, It's Only You. I'm fine. More to the point, how are you feeling after your little scare last night?"

She relaxed in her chair as she listened to Simon's soothing voice. She loved his Scottish accent, which was one of the things that had attracted her to him. They had known each other for over five years before either of them had shown any real interest in the other. She kicked herself under the table for wasting so much time, but then she reminded herself she had a good enough excuse for not getting involved sooner: she'd been married to Darryl at the time. Her ex's evil features filled her mind, and she shuddered. Pushing Darryl aside as quickly as he'd appeared, she replied, "We had a good night. I let Dex sleep on the bed last night as a special treat. When I woke up this morning, he was still curled up beside me, sleeping peacefully."

"Hmm... am I allowed to be jealous of a dog?"

Sally groaned. "Gosh, don't say that..."

"Hey, are you all right? I was only teasing."

"I know. It doesn't matter, honestly. It's just the past emerging. Darryl used to be jealous of everything that got too close to me, including Dex, which is why he lived with Mum and Dad for a while."

"No! I'm so sorry. I had no idea, Sal. What a bloody moron. You're best shot of him."

"When I was drifting off to sleep last night, I was reflecting on what Dex went through, and his name cropped up. If he wasn't in prison now, I wouldn't have put it past him to do that to my boy.

He's warped, a twisted fucker. If only I hadn't fallen for his charming, manipulative ways... sorry, I'm prattling on."

"Hey, if it helps to vent then vent away. Fancy dinner tonight?"

"Well... I hate to put Dex first, but would you mind if we left it for another day?"

"Tomorrow then?"

She blew out a relieved breath—she hadn't detected a note of rejection in his voice. He really was one in a million.

"Sod it, go on then. Tonight would be lovely. Besides, I missed not seeing you last night."

"Ha, well, you know what the solution to that is. No pressure on my part, of course."

"I know. I just need to get used to the idea. Be patient with me."

"Hey, after what you've been through in the past, that's a no-brainer. I will say one thing in my defence, if I may?"

"Go on."

"I might not have had that many relationships, but I've always treated the women I've dated with the utmost respect, and I meant what I said the other day. It took a lot to ask you to share my home. I've never given anyone else that option before."

Her heart began pounding rhythmically. "I know, I appreciate the offer, and just to reiterate, I didn't flat-out reject it. Blame my screwed-up head if that helps."

"Let's hope your heart has a word with your head and you come to the right decision in the end. Oops... my assistant needs me. I'm going to have to love you and leave you."

"Okay. Shall I meet you at the usual restaurant at seven?"

"Marvellous. If anything changes, I'll ring you. Have a good day."

"You, too." Sally ended the call, sipped her coffee, and contemplated the evening ahead of her with a huge smile on her face. *This is what love should feel like! Not what I experienced during my sham of a marriage.*

After finishing her drink, she whizzed through the post and paperwork she had neglected for the past day or so. Relieved and satisfied that it was out of the way, she could concentrate all her efforts on finding the killer who had left behind three victims.

Cold Case

Sally sent Jordan out for sandwiches and cakes to boost the team's fading morale as twelve thirty approached. Just after lunch, they gathered around the incident board and highlighted what they'd discovered that morning, which really wasn't much to shout about.

Sally tutted. "Okay, so Jack and I will get on with interviewing the family members and friends of all three victims this afternoon. I need you guys to keep digging into Warren Dean's past."

"That's a lot of people we have to interview, boss. I'm not averse to taking on all that responsibility, but it makes more sense to split the work up. Leave one member of the team here while four of us go out and about."

She knew Jack was talking sense, however, Sally was eager to question all the individuals herself. "Okay, well, you know how much of a control freak I am. It was a rhetorical question, guys," she added quickly as several of her colleagues opened their mouths to speak. "I realise we're against time here, so I'm willing to let Joanna and Stuart visit the burglars' families. Good compromise, yes?"

Everyone nodded their acceptance.

"Remember that our priority remains searching for something that links the three victims. I want to know why Wilson and Jenkinson turned to crime in the first place and why they continued to rob their community."

"Yes, boss," Joanna replied, jotting down Sally's instructions.

"Jack, you and I are going to pay Aisha's father a visit. I haven't finished that line of enquiries just yet. I'm a little annoyed that he hasn't at least picked up the phone to make contact with us."

~ ~ ~

Mr. Maqsood's grocery store was in the small village of Knotley, about a ten-minute commute from the couple's home. Sally parked the car in the lay-by, then she and Jack left the car and approached the shop. Outside, a vast array of fruit and veg, all top quality, not a brown leaf or bruise in sight, was on display. The man obviously cared about the produce he offered to the public. Stepping inside the store, Sally's first assumption of the store owner proved to be an accurate one. Quickly surveying the shelves, she was amazed to see nothing out of place and all the products were set in precise lines with the product names facing forwards.

"Neatest small store I've ever seen," Sally whispered.

"Yeah, I was thinking the same. Some would say the person might be a little obsessed with how things look."

"I'd be inclined to think along those lines, too."

They walked to the end of the first row of shelves and found a Middle Eastern man in his mid-fifties to early sixties sitting behind the counter, smiling at them. He hopped off his stool and approached the counter between them.

"Hello, Mr. Maqsood. I'm DI Sally Parker, and this is my partner, DS Jack Blackman. Is it all right if we have a quiet word with you?" Sally showed the man her warrant card.

He leaned forward to study her ID, the smile on his face long forgotten. When his eyes met Sally's again, a darkness appeared in his features. "Ah, yes, you are the two detectives who visited my home and upset my wife."

"I'm sorry she felt that way. It wasn't our intention. All we're trying to do is track down the person responsible for your daughter's death. I thought you would both appreciate that."

"Why? Ten years ago this happened. Why revisit the case now?" His gaze narrowed as he rested his hands, which were balled into tight fists, on the counter in front of him.

"As I explained to your wife the other day, new evidence has come to our attention. Forgive me, but I really don't understand why you're both so uptight about this. Surely, any parent would want closure for their child's death, don't you?"

"Of course we want closure. I just don't understand why it has taken ten years for you lot to start reinvestigating the case. I hope that husband of hers is at the top of your suspect list, because last time, it was as though he never existed."

"He's up there, along with everyone else we've interviewed so far."

His eyes turned to tiny slits. "*Everyone* else? Are you including my wife in that sweeping statement, Inspector?"

Sally shrugged. "Like I said, everyone is on the list until we have evidence to prove their innocence."

He raised one of his hands, pointed his finger and waved it from side to side. "Now wait just a minute. I think you have that the wrong way round. Shouldn't you be investigating this crime with the intention of proving someone's guilt?"

"I tend to look at things differently. I like to delve deeper when I investigate, to prove a person is either innocent or guilty, sir. It's why I've never failed to apprehend, arrest and imprison a guilty person. If during that process I tick people off, then there is very little I can do about that."

"You should be ashamed of yourself saying that."

"Why? The results speak for themselves. The only people who should be against the way I tackle a case are the guilty parties. Are you placing yourself in that category, sir?"

He huffed. "Don't be so absurd. What are my wife and I supposed to be guilty of?" His tone was becoming more irate, and with it, his accent was getting thicker.

"You tell me," she said, calling his bluff.

"I don't like the inference you're making, Inspector. My wife loved our daughter deeply. We would never harm a hair on her head."

"Glad to hear it. May I ask why you haven't contacted me in the last forty-eight hours?"

"Did you tell me to? My wife didn't inform me. So, because I neglected to contact you, you believe that it is a sign of my guilt. Is that what you're saying?"

"Not at all. However, I was expecting you to contact me, especially if, as in your words, I upset your wife when I questioned her the other day."

His mouth opened and shut several times as if he were a gasping fish out of water. Finally, he growled, "Look around you. I manage this shop by myself. You think it looks this good just from me sitting behind a counter all day? I'm here from six in the morning until ten at night. You think I have time to chase after an officer who is intent on blaming a victim's family for her death?"

Sally raised a hand. "Now wait just a minute. I never said anything of the sort. It's my job to reinvestigate this crime to the best of my ability. I've already uncovered several things that the original officer in charge of the case either missed or chose to ignore. I have to tell you that all your anger is doing is raising my suspicions more. Now, why don't you tone down your anger and start being civil to me? After all, I'm only trying to find out who hated your daughter enough to want to take her last breath."

His head hung low in shame, he mumbled, "I'm sorry. I thought you were pointing the finger in my wife's and my direction." He looked her in the eye. "That, I swear, is all I'm guilty of. I see it so often."

Sally's brow wrinkled in confusion. "See what?"

"Miscarriage of justice. All people in this country see at present is the colour of our skin. Since Brexit has happened, people who have lived in this country—I'm talking about my fellow countrymen here—have been rated as second-class citizens. That is why I'm guilty of being defensive, and my wife, come to that. Please forgive us, Inspector."

"Apology accepted. I'm sorry for any trouble you've experienced lately. But please, all I'm doing is trying to close this case. I want to see whoever is guilty of killing your daughter and two other victims brought to justice and rotting behind bars."

"What? Two other victims? I'm unaware of this. Why have I not been told about this before?"

"It's only just come to our attention, Mr. Maqsood. The new evidence I referred to proves that the two suspects the original officer earmarked as killing your daughter were also killed around that time."

He shook his head, looking confused. "I don't understand. How can that be?"

"We've yet to determine the ins and outs. All I can say is that I won't stop investigating this case until the culprit has been identified and found. You have my word on that, sir."

"I appreciate that, Inspector. I'm sorry again for my bad behaviour. For the past ten years, my wife and I have been riddled with guilt."

"Why? Aisha's death was beyond your control. There's no need for you to feel guilty."

"Do you have any children, Inspector?"

Sally shook her head.

Cold Case

"Deep down, a parent will always feel a failure if they have been unable to protect their child. I know we weren't there at the time, but that feeling of frustration and helplessness lingers on. It will live with us until our dying day, until we're reunited with Aisha."

Unexpected tears sprang to Sally's eyes. She felt remorseful for ever thinking Aisha's parents could have been guilty of killing her. "I hope the pain and guilt lessen over time, sir. Maybe once we can supply you with closure, those feelings of guilt will disappear altogether."

"I hope so, Inspector, but I fear they never will."

"We'll be in touch soon, I hope."

"Thank you. I appreciate you taking on the case. It makes a difference to know that our daughter's case is being treated with consideration this time around."

"Goodbye, sir."

Both Sally and Jack shook his hand before turning to leave. Once they were back in the car, Sally struggled to hold back the tears and even heard Jack gulping a few times beside her. "It's all so sad, Jack. What a waste of a life."

"What's up, boss? This is so unlike you to break down like this."

On the return journey to the station, she relayed the events of what Dex had been subjected to the night before.

"What? And you didn't see anyone else around?"

"Nope, only the other dog owner who helped me look for him."

"Maybe it was him."

Sally pulled into the station car park and swivelled in her seat to look at him. "No way! He helped me rescue Dex, tore the tape off his muzzle, and cut the bindings from his legs. Why on earth would you think he'd do such a cruel thing as that?"

"I've known crazier things to happen, Sally. Ask yourself this question: do you carry a penknife in your pocket for emergencies?"

"No, because that's a man thing to do, not something us women think of doing."

He tilted his head and raised a questioning eyebrow. "It is? I don't carry one around with me."

Sally shook her head in disbelief. "I don't believe it. No, you've got to be wrong, Jack."

He shrugged and pulled the handle on the car door. "Have you seen this man around your neck of the woods before?" He exited the car.

Sally got out and stared at him over the roof. "No, I've never seen him before. All right, I'll go along with your theory that maybe it was him. Tell me why?"

"How the hell do I know? You know what weird and wonderful people are walking our streets today. Mostly, there's no rhyme or reason behind half the crimes that are committed. These idiots do it for the sheer hell of it."

She locked the car and walked towards the entrance of the station. Shaking her head, she said, "But another dog owner? A pet lover?"

"Maybe he borrowed the dog to lure Dex away from you."

"Either you have a very warped imagination, or you're spot on. I hope it's the former. Look, Dex is all right. I'd rather forget all about the incident now."

"Just as a precaution, perhaps you should reconsider where you walk Dex from now on."

"I've already considered that."

CHAPTER TEN

Around forty-five minutes before Sally and Jack were due to leave to interview the teachers, Joanna and Jordan returned, looking triumphant.

Sally propped herself on the desk closest to Joanna. "Get on with it. You've clearly found out something important. What is it?"

Joanna removed her coat and sat down. "We think we might have come up with a possible connection, boss."

Sally's eyes widened, and she leaned forward. "Do tell."

"After chatting to both men's relatives, the wife of Wilson and the ex-wife of Jenkinson, they confirmed that the men owed money to a loan shark in the area."

Sally's brow furrowed. "Okay, that might connect the two burglars and be the reason behind them turning to burgling their neighbourhood, but how does that link Aisha to them?"

"That's the part we need to figure out, boss. Maybe we should ask Patrick Thomas if he'd been in touch with this loan shark."

Sally cupped her chin thoughtfully. "Worth a shot. It can't do any harm. Jack and I need to make a move soon. I'll seek him out in the morning. What else did the women have to say?"

"Jenkinson's ex-wife was very unhelpful, couldn't wait to get rid of us, which is understandable considering she's the ex. That was the reason behind their divorce—because he'd saddled them with a huge debt, plus he'd gone behind her back and borrowed money off the loan shark. They ended up losing the house because of it."

"People get so desperate these days. Instead of cutting back and saving up for what they can't have, all they do is spend what they haven't got and put the rest on credit they can't afford to repay." Sally tutted. "Hark at me, I sound like my mother." Even her parents had fallen into the trap of accumulating a debt they couldn't cover. That hadn't been self-inflicted, however, as her father had carried out some building work for a man who absconded the country before paying her father's invoice. That was why Sally had taken over their mortgage and was living back at home. If she hadn't, the building society would have repossessed the house, and Sally would never have forgiven herself if that happened.

Joanna nodded. "I agree, boss, which is why I refuse to have a credit card."

"Me, too. They're the curse of our generation. A friend of mine built a house and ran out of money so started slamming it on her card. She ended up with a twenty-grand debt. Anyway, that's beside the point. What about Mrs. Wilson? Was she saddled with a huge debt, too?"

"Yes, she told me she's still trying to pay it off today. Fortunately, she's remarried, and her new husband is helping her to repay the instalments every month."

"Bloody hell, he's an understanding sort. Had she been informed that her former husband's body has been discovered?"

"Yes, boss. She seemed a little upset, maybe relieved even. But said she's more than happy with the hand she had been dealt, and that she's now married to a lovely, caring, law-abiding man, who she wouldn't be without."

"That's lovely to hear. Glad she has moved on with her life and everything is working out for her. I take it the ex, Mrs. Jenkinson was less forgiving by what you've told me already."

Joanna nodded. "As soon as I mentioned her ex's name, she began shouting a lot of expletives, calling him some unsavoury names. Not sure how I kept a straight face when she called him a cockwomble!"

"A what?" Sally laughed.

"Precisely. It sounded so funny at the time. Anyway, her final words were, 'I hope he rots in hell'. Do you want me to chase up the loan shark while you're out?"

"If you would, do some digging, and Jack and I will set off in the morning to try and confront the bastard if he's still operating in the area."

"I seemed to recall the name when the ladies mentioned it. Spike Barker."

Cold Case

"Hmm... the name also rings a bell with me. Find out what you can. Good work, Joanna and Jordan. We better shoot off now, or if we're late, the teachers might force us to stay behind and put us in detention."

~ ~ ~

Sally and Jack arrived at the school with five minutes to spare. Sally had attended Highfield School herself as a teenager, and she had mixed feelings as she walked through the gates and entered the winding corridors that led to the music department. She had enjoyed most of her lessons, with the exception of geography, which she truly detested. Maybe it was because of the madcap things her geography teacher used to say during his classes. But it was the memory of being hounded by a small group of bullies that saddened her. The girls, all her own age of fourteen, had ruled the school playground. They hadn't just singled out one of the pupils, they had shared their unwanted attention around the whole class, including the boys. One day they picked on the wrong person—a girl called Virginia Sandalwood, who had taken up karate after school. Sally had witnessed the day Virginia caught the gang picking on a girl named Christine, who had a hearing defect. Virginia went nuts, and beginning with the leader, she tore into the five girls in the group, leaving them in a heap. Sally had intervened to prevent Virginia from attacking the bullies further. The bullies got to their feet and bolted before Virginia could continue her assault. They had never had the guts to try it on with any other pupil after that day.

"Why are you smiling?" Jack asked, looking sideways at her.

"Just remembering the good times I used to have around here."

"Wow, I didn't realise you went to this school. How was it? My parents sent me to an all-boys' school."

"We had our ups and downs, but mostly, I had a really good time here."

"I hated my school days. No fun without girls being around to tease."

Sally swiped his arm. "Men!"

They rounded the corner to find a woman with purple hair and wearing half-moon glasses leaning against a doorframe. "Well it's about time; you're late. I'm Pamela Albright, head of the music department."

Sally glanced at her watch. "Only two minutes late. Sorry for the inconvenience. Is everyone here?"

"Yes, well, except Jonathon Drake. He sent his apologies, as he has a dentist appointment at four fifteen."

"That's a shame. We'll have to catch up with him another day then."

"Sorry I have to ask, but I need to see your formal IDs. Can't be too careful today, can we?"

Sally and Jack both produced their warrant cards and held them in front of the woman's face. After scrutinising them, she nodded and pushed open the door behind her. "These are Sandra Ball and Lisa Atkins. Both ladies worked alongside Aisha Thomas before... well, before she died."

"Okay, we'd like to interview you all separately. We shouldn't take long, just a brief chat to ask what you can remember about your time working with Aisha and what you know about the incident surrounding her death."

"Just a minute." Mrs. Albright stepped out into the corridor and returned a few seconds later. "The room opposite is free. Use this room for interviews, and the rest of us can wait in the room opposite."

"Fantastic. Who wants to go first?" Sally asked, smiling at the teachers.

The women all glanced at each other and shrugged.

Finally, Lisa Atkins raised her hand. "I'll go first if you want?"

"Thank you. Ladies, if you wouldn't mind leaving the room, we shouldn't be too long."

Pamela and Sandra walked swiftly from the room. Jack assembled the chairs around the large teacher's desk at the front of the classroom.

"First of all, I'd like to thank you for agreeing to see us at short notice, Lisa. Can you tell me how well you knew Aisha Thomas?"

"Very well. She was my best friend at work, and we even met up a few times after school, too."

"Excellent. Maybe you can give us a little insight into her personality? To date, we've only questioned members of her family, and they can be a tad biased, as you can imagine."

"Okay. She was a lovely girl, very caring and compassionate with her pupils. You know she offered extra tutoring to the more talented students after school hours, right?"

"We'd heard something along those lines. So she was dedicated to her job, in other words?"

"Extremely dedicated to her work. In fact, I've never met another teacher so dedicated to her students. It was a great loss to lose not just a friend, but a talented teacher, also."

"I'm sure. As a personal friend, did she ever confide in you?"

"All the time. Was there anything specific you need to know about?"

"Did she ever say what her marriage was like? Did Patrick and Aisha get along well?"

"Very well. They were extremely happy, considering what they had to put up with from her parents. They despised him. Maybe that came out wrong—I don't think her parents despised him per se, more the fact that she married someone outside of her own culture and religion. I hope that doesn't sound racist, voicing that. You never can tell nowadays, can you?"

"No, I don't think it sounded racist, just factual. They never fell out about anything?"

Lisa stared over Sally's shoulder at the blackboard behind her for a moment or two before she replied. "Not that I know of. They genuinely were a very happy couple. He did shift work being a copper, so perhaps them not being around each other all the time helped on that front."

"Maybe you're right there." Sally laughed. "Did Aisha ever mention if they had any money problems at all?"

Lisa shook her head and frowned. "No, never. Did she? Have money troubles, I mean?"

"We're not sure. Some evidence has come our way connecting Aisha's death with another two deaths around that time, and we're searching for a possible link. That's all."

"You mean she was killed by a serial killer?"

"Possibly. That's not for public knowledge yet. What about Patrick's parents? Did they get on with Aisha? Do you know?"

"As far as I know. She tended to cling to them a little because she missed her own mother and father so much. It was all rather upsetting for the poor girl. I tried my best to reassure her that it wasn't her fault and that I thought her parents were overreacting, but she merely shook her head and said, 'You don't understand what damage I've done to my family by marrying Patrick.'"

"Do you think Aisha was regretting her decision?"

"I'm not sure that's the case. She was extremely sad that she was unable to see her parents and to talk them around. I hope they're riddled with guilt for letting her down. Families should never disown each other like that. It's not as if she killed anyone. Sorry, that was the wrong thing to say, but you get my drift. She married a man she fell in love with. Nothing is set in stone in this life, and she saw a chance for happiness and grabbed it with both hands. She couldn't have realised how much damage saying yes to Patrick would do. Her whole family was ripped to shreds, and she was inconsolable about that."

"It is very sad. To answer your question, yes, I think her parents feel an element of guilt, not that they would admit it to anyone. They're still beside themselves after all these years."

"That's sad, and yet it's what they deserve for treating her so appallingly."

"Life is full of regrets. Let's just say I believe her parents have a few. What about around here? Was she liked by all the staff and the pupils? Perhaps we should be interviewing some of the parents she had fallen out with."

Lisa shuffled in her seat, and her gaze drifted over her shoulder at the closed door before she leaned in and whispered, "I'm not really one for telling tales, but Sandra had issues with Aisha."

Sally turned to face Jack, raised an eyebrow, and motioned for him to take notes. "Sandra Ball?"

Lisa nodded.

"What kind of issues are we talking about?"

"I'm only saying this for Aisha's sake. The last thing I want is for Sandra to get into trouble."

"I can't guarantee that. Please tell us what their relationship was like?"

"Well, before Aisha arrived at the school, Sandra used to be the type of person everyone went to for advice about a pupil or if they wanted to go down a certain route teaching a child. She enjoyed giving that advice, saw herself as a deputy head of the department, I suppose."

"And that status changed when Aisha began working at the school?"

"Yes. Aisha was a wonderful, caring person, unlike Sandra. She's... well, I guess the term I would use is *officious*. You know the type."

Sally nodded. "I do, indeed. Go on."

"The children used to be drawn to Aisha like a magnet. They looked forward to attending her classes because they always learnt something new and knew that Aisha would have the patience to explain their faults without screaming at them, unlike..." She motioned with her head towards the door.

"I completely understand. Thinking back to when I was at school, it was the gentle, caring teachers who got the most out of me. So that pissed... sorry, ticked Sandra Ball off?"

"Completely. In the staff canteen, I'd often see her glaring at Aisha. I swear she didn't deserve that. You truly couldn't wish to meet a nicer person."

"Well, someone had a grudge against Aisha, because they set out to kill her."

Lisa gasped, and her hand covered her mouth for a moment before it dropped into her lap again. "So it wasn't a burglary gone wrong, like the investigating officer back then insinuated?"

"No, the new evidence has totally put that line of enquiry to bed."

"Goodness me, why on earth would someone intentionally target a beautiful, talented person like Aisha?"

"At this point, we really have no idea."

"After all I've told you about Sandra, I really don't think she would be capable of killing anyone."

"It depends what buttons were pressed by Aisha. Did they have any particular argument that sticks in your mind?"

"Let me think... one time really stands out. Sandra confronted Aisha about taking one of the more talented students away from her. It was daft really; the student wanted extra piano training, and Sandra couldn't squeeze her into her busy schedule. As the student was entering a regional competition, Aisha bent over backwards, adjusted her schedule to suit the student. As you can imagine, Sandra was livid because she thought it showed that she didn't care as much as Aisha. Which was true, by the way. Sandra hated the way all the talented students were drawn to Aisha and not to her."

"That must have stuck in Sandra's throat. Can you tell me what her mood was like back then compared to now?"

"She's far more relaxed now that Aish... well, now that Aisha is no longer with us. It all came across as rather childish to me, but because Sandra had been here the longest, nothing was done about it."

"Are you telling me that the head of the department was aware of the conflict?"

"Oh yes, everyone in the bloody school was aware of it, even the pupils."

"Do you think the pupils initiated anything intentionally? Tried to play one off against the other?"

"Would kids be capable of doing that, Inspector?"

"I don't know really. Isn't it what they do with their parents all the time?"

"I've never thought about it that way. I suppose some of them might possibly be guilty of that, but I couldn't name any names."

"No, that's fine. Perhaps you can tell me a little about Sandra's background. Is she married, for instance?"

"Yes, at least she used to be. She divorced her husband around five years ago."

"Do you know why the marriage failed?"

"I think he went off with his secretary. That was the rumour I heard. Maybe you should ask her that."

"I will, thank you. And you say that she's a much calmer person around here nowadays?"

"Yes. Maybe ditching the husband has more to do with that than Aisha not being at the school now."

"Maybe. We'll see what she says."

"What about the parents of these talented children? Could one of them have had a grievance with Aisha that might have spiralled out of control at any time?"

Lisa thought over the question again and clicked her fingers. "I seem to recall one tiny incident which occurred after school one day."

Sally sat forward to the edge of her seat. "I'm listening."

"One of the mothers arrived to pick up her son. He'd forgotten to tell her that Aisha was giving him extra piano instruction that evening. She marched through the corridors and burst into the music room. I was in the room at the time; she didn't see me initially. She stormed up to Aisha, who was sitting next to her son on the piano stool, and slapped her hard around the face. I stepped forward and stood between Aisha and the woman before anything further could take place."

"That's strange. Why did the woman slap Aisha?"

"She screamed that Aisha was grooming her son. Nothing, nothing could have been further from the truth. Aisha, never ever laid a hand on any of the children at this school. She wasn't the type, for God's sake."

"Can you remember the woman's name?"

"I'm hardly likely to forget it. Mrs. Dawn Ward."

"Would you be able to supply us with her address?"

"I think so. I'll go and look in the secretary's office at the files from back then after I'm finished here."

"Wonderful. Going back to the incident, can you tell me how Aisha reacted to the assault? Did she complain to the headmaster or mistress or file an assault charge at the police station?"

Lisa's brow furrowed as she thought. "I know I called a halt to the tuition that day and escorted the woman and her child off the premises. When I returned, Aisha was sobbing her heart out. We both ended up in tears. Our role as teachers is to nurture our students, not bloody abuse them. What Mrs. Ward's logic was behind the accusation is beyond me. She said nothing when I walked her out to her car. Mind you, she probably saw how livid I was so thought it would be best to keep quiet."

"Do you know if Aisha told her husband?"

"She didn't say anything to me. After that day, Aisha never mentioned the vile incident again."

"Did anything else happen after that day?"

"I know what you're getting at, and yes, Aisha changed. She stopped tutoring the students after school, said if she wasn't being appreciated, then why should she put herself out. It wasn't as if she got paid for it. She did it because she felt proud of seeing the students flourish."

"Can you remember how long after the incident occurred that Aisha lost her life?"

"It was only a matter of a few weeks, I believe." Tears welled up in her bright-green eyes.

"That's very sad. Would you say that Aisha became withdrawn?"

"I suppose you could put it that way. Although the day she died, a group of us had arranged to go out for a meal and to see a show. That invitation had pulled her out of the doldrums, and she seemed like her old self once more. We were devastated when she didn't turn up that evening. I dropped by the house later on, and that's when Patrick told me what had gone on. I was in shock for weeks. She had such a beautiful soul, and all the people around her tried to damage her in one way or another."

"By that you mean Sandra, Mrs. Ward and Aisha's parents? What about the husband?"

"No. Patrick loved his wife; any idiot could see that. They were meant to be together. Soulmates. It proves it because he's never moved on, as far as I know. He's a good-looking man. Dozens of women out there would feel honoured to be in his life. He just can't get over Aisha."

"And you know that for a fact? You've spoken to him since her death?"

"Yes, he confided in me a few times after the funeral. I gave him my number and told him that if he ever needed to chat to ring me, night or day. Derek didn't mind at the beginning, but once Patrick rang at midnight. We were in bed asleep, and my husband answered the phone and shouted at Patrick to leave us alone. I was furious with Derek. He had no right to speak to him like that. I tried to ring Patrick to apologise the next day, but he refused to accept my call. I rang a few times. The last time, his partner answered his mobile and told me to 'back off' and that 'Patrick didn't need me hanging around reminding him of what he'd lost'. So that's what I did: backed off and never made contact with him again."

"I'm sorry that happened. Patrick seems to have come to terms with his wife's death over the years. Maybe he threw himself into his job more to avoid having a social life and getting involved with anyone else."

"Maybe. It's a shame, though. I would have preferred to have stayed in contact with him, offering my support."

Sally glanced at her watch and sighed. "Time's marching on. Is there anything else you think we should know?"

"I think we've covered everything. I hope I haven't got anyone into trouble."

"You haven't. If you can get me Mrs. Ward's address and send Sandra in for a chat on your way out, I'd appreciate it."

Sally watched Lisa walk out of the room. "All very interesting, eh, Jack?"

"The suspect list is certainly growing, boss. The question is: are any of them likely killers?"

"Yeah, all these interviews are making our job harder instead of easier, that's for sure. Let's see what Sandra has to say for herself."

The woman flounced into the room, plonked herself into the chair opposite, and folded her arms before Jack could reply.

"Hello again, Sandra. Sorry to keep you waiting so long."

"I hope this won't take an eternity. Some of us have a home to go to and a life to lead, Inspector." Sandra glared at Sally, and the corner of her eye twitched in what appeared to be anger.

The hair on the back of Sally's neck stood on end, the way it always did when she either didn't trust someone or took an instant dislike to a person. She wasn't sure which category Sandra belonged in yet. "We'll try not to take up too much of your time, I promise. Perhaps you can tell us what your relationship with Aisha Thomas was like?"

"Relationship? Do you mean friendship?"

"I stand corrected—your friendship." Sally was seething, saw the correction as a time-wasting exercise by the woman. Lisa was right. The woman did come across as being too damn officious.

"Let's say that we tolerated each other."

"Tolerated? In other words, you disliked her. That's what I perceive the word to mean. Why, when everyone else seemed to get on with her?"

"There are some people in this life that no matter how hard you try, you still can't make friends with them."

"Is that how things panned out with you and Aisha?"

"Yes, I suppose so. I tried on several occasions to have a conversation with the woman, but she turned her nose up at me and said that she wasn't at school to make friends with people. Huh! That wasn't the case with the rest of the staff. She seemed on good terms with all of them."

"So you felt left out. Is that right?"

Sandra's eyes drifted down to the desk in between them as she unfolded her arms and placed her hands in her lap. "Maybe. Wouldn't you? If all your colleagues excluded you from their banter in the staffroom?"

"I've never found myself in that position, so I really couldn't say. Did you try and heal the rift between you?"

"On more than one occasion, but she ignored me. Over time, I learnt to accept we were never going to be good friends and went on with my life."

"That must have been hard to deal with. Did your colleagues empathise with you?"

Sandra's head rose. She looked Sally in the eye and nodded. "Some did. Some chose to be on her side."

"They took sides? Are you kidding me? I know this is a school, but surely what you're describing is playground behaviour."

"Call it what you like. I've never fallen out with any of my other colleagues over the years."

"So why Aisha? Because of her colour?"

Sandra's eyes bulged. "Definitely not. How dare you call me a racist—how bloody *dare* you?"

Sally turned to Jack. "Did I mention the word *racist*?"

"No, boss, you merely asked a question if the woman's colour had anything to do with Ms. Ball's reluctance to get along with Aisha at school."

Sally supressed the laugh tickling her throat. She was glad to see that Jack was paying attention to her line of questioning. "That's right. I believe you twisted my words, Sandra. Please answer my question."

"I'm sorry, but that's how it came across to me. It had nothing to do with her skin colour. It was more about a personality clash. It's not unheard of, you know, in a workplace."

"I'm aware of that, thank you. From what we can gather, Aisha was a caring and kind person. Can you tell me what traits you saw in her that warranted the way you treated her?"

"Treated her? I didn't treat her any differently to the other members of staff here. We simply didn't get on."

Sally sighed heavily. "I'm trying to ascertain the reason *why* you didn't get on. You're the one who wishes to get home quickly, Ms. Ball. I suggest you stop dancing around the issue and be honest with me."

"I *have* been honest with you. I've said it was a clash of personalities. Why do you insist on going over the same questions?"

"I wasn't aware that I've been repeating myself. All I want to know is why you didn't get along with Aisha and yet everyone else did."

Sandra inhaled a deep breath and folded her arms once again. "The day she stepped through the main entrance, she took over. The music department was doing very well before she came along."

"Ah, so you were jealous of her. Is that what this was all about? Because the students preferred her type of tutoring to yours?"

"Not at all. Every teacher is different."

"Yes, but according to what we've heard already, you were like the deputy head of the department and got shoved down the pecking order not only by the staff, but by the students also. Is that right?"

"No, and you wait, I'll give that Lisa a piece of my mind for leading you down the wrong path."

Sally leaned back in her chair and folded her arms. "Then why don't you tell us in your own words what type of 'friendship' you and Aisha had."

Sandra inhaled a large breath, and her eyes narrowed in annoyance. "I really can't see what this has to do with anything. However, I'm willing to tell you so that I can get home this evening."

"Very wise. It'll save us calling you in to have an interview at the station," Sally said with a taut grin.

"Okay, it's sort of true. Aisha and I didn't always see eye to eye over how she carried out her tuition, but there are plenty of other teachers in this school I don't see eye to eye with, too. I doubt I'm the only teacher in that situation, either."

"But why didn't you agree with her teaching methods, especially if the children were keen on her teaching them?"

"I have a strict way of doing things to get the best out of the children. Let's just say that Aisha's way was more relaxed."

"And you came down heavy on her for that?"

"I didn't 'come down heavy on her'. I simply didn't agree with it."

"Why? Because the pupils preferred her teaching method to yours?"

Sandra glared at Sally. "I wouldn't say that at all. I had just as many pupils requesting my help as she did."

"Really? Maybe we'll clarify that with the head of the department when we speak to her after you."

She shrugged. "Do what you like."

Sally sat forward. "Why the attitude, Sandra? All I'm trying to find out is how Aisha fit in around here."

"I don't have an attitude. I'm annoyed that Lisa has sullied my name. I tried to get on with Aisha for months. She was never willing to meet me halfway."

"Why should she? Is it obligatory that everyone should get on around here? In every workplace—because I know damn well that I don't get on with all my work colleagues—it doesn't hamper the way we go about our jobs, though."

"If teachers don't get on, then the pupils pick up on any tension flying around and can use it against us."

"Is that what happened? Wouldn't your pupils stick to attending your classes and Aisha's stick with hers? Isn't that how it works? Or do you teach the pupils in different subjects? Sorry if I sound confused."

"No, you're right. The pupils were taught by either one of us, not both of us. I meant that kids talk in the playground. They can be very poisonous in nature, too."

Sally's head tilted, and frowning, she turned to Jack. "Am I missing something here?"

His mouth turned down at the sides, and he shook his head. "If you're missing it, then so am I, boss."

Sally turned back to the fidgeting Sandra. "Would you care to elaborate on that?"

"Why do I have to spell everything out to you? Kids talk, that's all I'm saying."

"I appreciate that, but unless they are given ammunition in the first place, why do you think you and Aisha were the talk of the playground? That's what's confusing me."

Sandra sighed and swept back a clump of her straight brunette hair. "Maybe a few of them overheard Aisha and me chatting one day."

"Chatting or arguing?"

"All right, having a disagreement, if you will."

"What about?"

"Her teaching methods. She was too soft with the kids."

"I've heard she was a devoted, very talented teacher who got the best out of her kids. Is that wrong?"

Sandra's chin dropped onto her chest.

When the woman didn't reply after a few moments, Sally had to prompt her again. "Sandra?"

Sandra looked up, her eyes widening in anger, matching her tone. "Yes, she was good with the pupils, but her methods sucked."

"You're not making sense, Ms. Ball."

"That's all I'm prepared to say on the matter. Are we finished?"

"Not quite. One last question, for now," Sally added, wanting to keep the uptight woman on her toes.

"Which is?"

"Did you attend Aisha's funeral?"

"What sort of question is that?"

"Did you?"

"No. Before you go reading anything sinister into that, the staff drew straws for who would go and who would stay here to keep the school running that day. I drew the short straw. I would have loved to have paid my respects to Aisha. I bore her no animosity whatsoever personally."

The way Sandra's eyes surprisingly moistened with tears made Sally believe her. "That's good to know. Okay, that will be all, Sandra, for now. We may need to question you further in the future."

Sandra rose from her chair and left the room.

"She was damn jealous of Aisha," Jack commented as the door closed behind the woman.

"Yep, that's my take on it, too. But would she set out to purposely harm Aisha physically?"

"Can't see it myself."

When they questioned Pamela Albright, she confirmed all that had been said and also stated that sometimes she had to tread carefully when both women were in the same room. Not because she felt Sandra was envious of the way the pupils flocked to Aisha and away from her. Sally asked Pamela if she thought that Sandra could have physically harmed Aisha, but the head of the music department was appalled by the question and refuted the claim outright.

When the interviews were over and it was time for Sally and Jack to leave, Lisa handed Sally the aggressive mother's address she had sought out, and Sally asked Mrs. Albright to supply, the missing teacher, Jonathon Drake's address.

Once she was back in the car, Sally noted the time on the dashboard. It was five forty-five already. "It's too late to go and see this Mrs. Ward now. We'll leave it until the morning, all right?"

"Fine by me. You want to drop me back to the station, or shall I catch a taxi?"

"I'll drop you back then shoot off. I have a date this evening."

Jack shook his head as Sally started the engine.

"What's that for?"

"I dread to think what you two discuss over dinner."

Sally laughed and pulled into the heavy flow of traffic. "You'd be surprised. Anyway, if this traffic doesn't ease soon, I might miss out on dinner altogether."

"Where are you going?"

"A little restaurant we always go to situated down by the river. It's always quiet during the week, bedlam at the weekend."

"Aww... an intimate dinner for two. Ain't that nice?"

"Stop being such a tease—or are you jealous because you and Donna never get the chance to go out for a meal?"

"You're probably right. I'm sure the kids would be all right if we left them alone for the evening, but Donna says she'd rather spend time at home with the family. It wouldn't be right going out on our own. Not that we can afford a slap-up meal somewhere on my pay."

"Get out of here. Forgo a few cans of beer now and then, and you'd soon save up enough for a nice meal somewhere."

"That, dear Sally, would be utter sacrilege. I need a few cans to unwind in the evening with my mob."

"And that is precisely why I don't intend having any children. The thought might have crossed my mind when I first got married, but it swiftly diminished. Not sure how you guys cope with working full time and then going home to start all over again. Give me a devoted dog to share my time with any day of the week."

"Maybe you've got a point. Let's see if your point of view alters when you and Simon get hitched. He seems a decent enough chap."

"It won't. He's too old to start wanting kids."

"Have you discussed it with him?"

"No, the conversation has never come up. Bloody hell, he only asked me to move in with him the other day." Sally bit down on her lip. She hadn't meant to blurt out that revelation. She'd wanted to keep the news to herself until she figured out what to do.

Jack twisted in his seat and stared at her. "Crikey, he didn't waste much time asking you that."

"Damn! That was supposed to be confidential. Not a word to anyone, Jack, right?"

"Do your parents know?"

"No. I'm not sure what's going to happen yet, Jack."

"Why the hesitation? Because of what you went through with that jerk, Darryl?"

"Possibly. I'm confused. I promised Mum and Dad that I would stick around and help out with the house. There's the mortgage to consider. I couldn't move in with Simon and expect him to keep me while I'm trying my hardest to keep a roof over Mum and Dad's heads. It wouldn't sit right with me. Then there's the boy wonder to think about. I don't want Dex being pulled around from pillar to post. He's settled with Mum and Dad, but I've grown used to having him around when I get home from work."

"Maybe consider having joint custody. Let your Mum and Dad have him on weekdays and you have him at the weekends."

"Hey, you might be onto something there. However, it doesn't solve the issue of sharing with Simon and what to do about the mortgage."

"You'll sort it. The real question you should be asking yourself is whether you're in love with Simon or not. If you are, all these doubts wouldn't be flying around, would they?"

Her cheeks warmed up as she pulled up alongside Jack's vehicle back at the station. "I think I love him, but I do have obvious reservations that I'm struggling with. Once upon a time, Darryl was just like Simon, and look how that turned out."

"Not all men are the same, Sal. Look at me. You don't think I go home every night and knock seven bells out of Donna, do you?"

She turned to face him. "Of course I don't."

"Then stop tarring all men with the same brush. I can understand your hesitancy and your inability at present to trust another man with your heart, but from where I'm standing, or sitting, I think Simon is a decent man who is probably guilty of devoting too much time to his job over the years. Has he had many girlfriends or even been married?"

"He's had a few—nothing major—and no, he's never been married. He said it took a lot for him to ask me to move in with him and that he's never felt the desire to ask anyone else he's dated over the years."

"There you go then. You're both highly intelligent people. My suggestion would be to air all your reservations with him and go from there. Living with each other will be full of compromises to begin with, you know that."

Sally leaned over and kissed his cheek. "Thanks, partner. You're a star for listening and offering a solution. Not every man could be bothered to do that."

"There you go tarring us all with that damn brush again. It's not going to be easy for you to make the right decision, given your past, but if you do go ahead and move in with him and things start to go wrong, make sure you let me know right away. I'll go round there and sort him out. Got that?"

"I hear you loud and clear. Thanks, Jack. Now get home to that adorable wife and wonderful family of yours. Say hi to them from me."

He winked and exited the vehicle. Sally pulled away immediately, knowing that she was twenty minutes away from home and the time was passing by rapidly.

CHAPTER ELEVEN

Sally eventually arrived home at six twenty-five. That gave her twenty minutes to fuss over Dex, say hello to her parents, and get ready for the evening. She would have to exchange her usual shower for a good wash and douse herself with plenty of smelly body lotion and perfume instead.

"Hello, boy. Have you had a good day?" She cuddled Dex amid his high-pitched moaning, and they both went through to the kitchen, where her mother and father were eating dinner. "Ooo... anything nice?"

"Something simple tonight as you're off out. Ham, egg and chips, your father's favourite."

Sally sat down at the table, pinched one of her father's chunky chips, and almost risked getting stabbed by his fork in the process. She looked at her mum. "I've said before, you don't have to bother about making a decent meal for me *every* single night, Mum. I don't expect it. Jacket spud, cheese and beans would do me occasionally."

"A working girl needs the appropriate sustenance, love. It's a pleasure cooking for you. Don't take that away from me."

Sally kissed her mother on the cheek. "I love you, but please take some time out for yourself. If ever you want to go out for a meal one evening, alone, just do it. I'm more than capable of fending for myself. Talking of which, I better get my skates on. I don't want to keep Simon waiting."

"You go, love. Enjoy yourself. No need to worry about Dex. Dad's taken him out for three long walks as it is today. He didn't let him off the lead after your fiasco yesterday."

She kissed her dad's head as she swept past him. "You're a treasure. Thanks, Dad."

"Get outta here. It's no hardship. I could do with losing this belly anyway." He pointed to the slight bulge to his tummy.

"Good luck with that, eating egg and chips." Sally ran out of the room before either of them could throw something at her. Dex rushed up the stairs alongside her and jumped on the bed. He watched her every move as she riffled through her wardrobe for something suitable to wear. His tail wagged when she pulled out a black skirt and a teal-blue sequined top.

"Too much bling, do you think?"

Dex barked a few times then laid his head on his paws. She had a quick strip-down wash in the bathroom and returned to find Dex lying in the same position. She couldn't resist placing her hands on either side of his cute face and kissing him on the head. He gave another high-pitched moan. Despite his protest, she knew he loved the affection she continually bestowed upon him. He was her baby, after all.

Five minutes later, she had dressed and reapplied her make-up. She was lucky she had unblemished skin and didn't need to apply a lot, unlike some women she saw on the streets of Norfolk.

Dex followed her back to the kitchen, where her parents were at the sink, washing and drying up the dishes together.

"I shouldn't be late back this evening. We have a lot on at work tomorrow."

"You look gorgeous, love. Have a wonderful time," her mother said, wearing a proud smile.

Her father nodded. "Enjoy yourself, love. Tell Simon we're looking forward to meeting him in a few days."

"I will. Love you."

Dex trotted along the hallway with her.

"You stay here and look after Mum and Dad for me, lovely."

His head dropped as she reached for the door catch to let herself out, and her heart broke in two. "I won't be long. I'll make it up to you tomorrow, I promise."

Simon was already seated at the table when the taxi dropped Sally off at the restaurant with a minute to spare. He stood up, hugged her tightly, and kissed her on the lips, then he held out the chair for her to sit down. He was such a gentleman.

"Have you had a busy day?" he asked, topping up her glass from the bottle of red he'd already started on.

"Very busy, without making much progress. What about you?"

"Pretty much the same. I won't go into detail, wouldn't want to put you off your meal."

"Great idea," she replied gratefully.

He clinked his glass against hers. "You look beautiful tonight. I'd be the envy of the restaurant, if it was full. To us!"

Sally looked around at the empty tables and laughed. "You old charmer, you."

"Not so much of the old, and I'm telling you the truth. I'm not in the habit of lying."

Sally felt her cheeks flare up. She took a sip of her wine and reached for his hand across the table. "Thank you. You're very sweet."

Simon shuddered and cringed. "That's the worst word you can use to describe a bloke, just for your information."

She laughed. "Seriously? Even though you are?"

He shuddered again. "Shall we change the subject? How is the case really going?"

Sally twirled her wineglass by the stem while she spoke. "Slowly. We've questioned a few people so far, and all that has successfully done is add to the suspect list."

"That's a good thing in a way, right?"

"Ordinarily, I'd agree with you. Not when you've only been given a month to solve the case, though."

"I see what you mean. Anything I can help with?"

"No, you've done your bit by dismissing the burglars for us, but you've also added to our workload by telling us that you believe all three victims were killed by the same method or same murderer. I don't suppose you've checked your records to make any other comparisons to any more victims that came into the pathology department around that time?"

"Good thinking. I could get one of my team to look into that tomorrow for you if it'll help. Maybe it will lead to more DNA evidence that will point to the killer."

"You never know. Stranger things have happened."

The waiter appeared at their table. "Are you ready to order?"

"Sorry, we've been chatting. Can you give us five minutes?" Simon said.

"Sure, it's not as if I'm rushed off my feet. Give me a nod when you're ready." He topped up their glasses before he left.

Sally and Simon picked up the menus and studied them. "I don't fancy steak. I want something different for a change. Any suggestions?" Sally said.

Simon glanced over the menu at her, a twinkle in his eye. "What about oysters? They're supposed to be an—"

"Aphrodisiac, I know, cheeky sod. You do know I'm going back to my place tonight?"

Simon looked down at his menu and mumbled, "You can't blame a man for trying."

She reached over and playfully slapped his hand. "You're a trier all right. I'll give you ten out of ten for that. Come on, help me out."

"What about something simple, like Hunter's chicken? It's smothered in a barbecue sauce and cheese."

"Sounds delicious. You've sold it to me."

Simon closed the menu, placed it on top of Sally's on the edge of the table, and called the waiter over. "Two Hunter's chicken, please."

"Good choice. It shouldn't be long."

The waiter left them alone, and Simon interlocked his fingers with hers. "I hate to bring this up—and please don't think I'm badgering you into making a decision—but have you thought over what I asked you the other day?"

Sally's eyes drifted down to their entwined fingers, and she swallowed. She would love nothing more than to say yes, however, all she could find were obstacles blocking their path. Even chatting with Jack earlier that evening hadn't resolved her dilemma. "Honestly?"

"Yes, honestly."

"I've thought about nothing else, when I haven't been distracted with the case, that is. Simon, I love you dearly and think you're a wonderful, caring man—"

"Why do I sense a huge *but* coming my way?"

"It's not a huge *but* at all. However, it is a plea for you to give me more time. If it'll help, I can talk through what's going on in my mind, but it would probably sound pathetic to you."

He shook his head. "If you have genuine reasons for not accepting my offer, then I'm happy to take them at face value and not to judge you at all. I'm aware of what you have gone through in the past. The trust element must be a major concern for you after what that scumbag did."

"Truly, it's not a matter of not trusting you—I do. The problem is that his nibs was a real charmer when I first met him and continued to be that way for the first few months we were married. Then one day, all that changed. He started telling me that he felt I was suffocating him. I wasn't. We barely saw each other, what with opposing work patterns. I think the thing he regretted most was me moving my stuff into his house. He used to say I was untidy, even if I was reading a book on the sofa."

"All I'm hearing is that this idiot was a selfish, spoilt brat. I repeat, I'm not like Darryl."

Sally cringed at the way he spat out her ex's name. Simon had never had the misfortune of meeting her ex, so he was only going by what she had relayed to him about Darryl. "I know you're not. If anything, you're the total opposite, but what if you object to me invading your space after a month or two?"

"I wouldn't," he replied, squeezing her hand as if to emphasise his point.

Sally's eyes unexpectedly welled up with tears. "But you can't guarantee that. Neither of us can."

"We'll work round it *if* it happens. I'm under no illusion that there won't be other compromises to be made, Sally, but surely, if we love each other, we'll be able to conquer any issues that come our way."

"I have no doubt we'll be able to overcome any differences coming our way, but that's not the only problem I can foresee."

He frowned. "Go on; you can't stop there."

"I made a commitment to my parents. I know that sounds strange. Even Jack thought it was silly me bringing it up when I discussed the matter with him earlier."

An amused grin pulled across his face. "You discussed my proposal with your partner? I'm not sure what to think about that."

"Oops, have I done something stupid? I just valued his opinion. He knows what I went through with my ex and how it affected me."

"So do I. I saw the bruises beneath the make-up you wore."

Sally withdrew her hand from his and gasped. "You did? And yet you never said anything."

"I told Jack to take care of you."

"He never told me that." She grabbed his hand once more.

"Anyway, that aside, I'm dying to know what Jack's take on it is."

"If you must know, he said I was being foolish and to go for it."

"Then your partner's common sense has rocketed in my estimation."

Sally chuckled. "It's more like you bloody men sticking together."

"So, what other concerns do you have?"

The conversation halted when the waiter appeared and placed their plates in front of them. "Enjoy your meals." He smiled before he disappeared.

"This looks scrummy," Sally said, her tummy grumbling at the smell wafting from her plate.

"Stop changing the subject. Come on, let's try and sort this out so we can move on."

Move on? Does that mean what I think it means? That if I reject his offer, he's going to dump me? She momentarily lost her appetite as a lump of panic lodged in her throat.

"Hey, you're not eating. Don't you like it?" Simon looked concerned.

"Yes, it's lovely. Okay, I'm just going to come out and ask. When you said 'move on', what exactly did you mean by that?"

He placed his knife and fork down and looked her in the eye. "Your face is a picture. I think we're on different wavelengths here, Sal. I just meant that we'll discuss it when we're further down the line. Did you think I was going to dump you?"

Her head dipped in shame. "Yes," she mumbled.

He placed a finger under her chin and raised her head. "Never. If there's any dumping going to happen, it'll be you that instigates it, not me."

The tension subsided in her shoulders, and she exhaled the breath she'd been holding in. "Thank goodness. Hey, maybe that little faux pas highlights how little we really know each other."

"Nonsense. Stop making excuses and eat your dinner."

Sniggering, she tucked into her meal and moaned with pleasure. "This really is superb."

"See? You really should trust my judgement."

"Okay, I have a question for you." He nodded for her to continue while he put a piece of barbecue-coated chicken in his mouth. "We've known each other—what? Four or five years? Why did it take you so long to ask me out?"

He almost choked on his chicken. "Well, that came out of the blue. Cards-on-the-table time it is then. I fancied you—is that how the kids put it?"

Laughing, she nodded, enjoying his embarrassing moment. "It is."

"I fancied you the first time I met you, but you were with Darryl back then. I kept tabs on what was going on with you once I saw you coming to work with bruises. Then when Jack told me that you and he had arrested Darryl, I had to bide my time before I asked you out. I knew your emotions would be in turmoil and you'd be unlikely to trust another man in the near future."

"So you had a spy, did you? Wait until I get my hands on that bloody underhanded partner of mine."

"Hey, I don't want him getting into trouble. Another reason I delayed asking you out was because I thought you'd knock me back."

"Why?"

"Apart from the trust issue, I thought you were too good for me. Look at you—you're a stunner. You can have your pick of any bloke out there."

Her heart pounded. "You're talking crap, but I appreciate your kind words. And do me a favour?"

"I'm deadly serious. You're beautiful. Go on, what favour?"

"Stop putting yourself down. After all, it was your good looks and your caring manner that sparked my interest in you in the first place."

His boyish face lit up. "Mind if I ask when that was exactly?"

"About the second time I met you."

"Bloody hell, really? You mean we've wasted four flipping years?"

"Hard to believe, but yes. We did have certain obstacles in our way, though."

He winked at her. "And look how well we've overcome them..."

"Like I said before, ten out of ten for trying. Bear with me. There's Mum and Dad to consider in this equation, not forgetting Dex, too."

"I know. I'm prepared to be patient. I can't wait to meet them on Sunday. Your dad's a builder, right?"

"Yep, he got screwed over by a client he was working for a few years ago, and that's where their money troubles began. I stepped in to help them out financially."

"That was honourable of you, Sal. Not every child would do that for their parents."

"I know, but the house would have been repossessed if I hadn't taken over the mortgage. That's a huge obstacle for me regarding your proposition. I couldn't afford to contribute to your household bills and keep running my family home."

"If that's all you're worried about, then don't be. I wouldn't expect you to contribute. I manage to run my house successfully myself, young lady, and that isn't going to change."

"I'm not a leech. I would have to pay my way, Simon. There might be some girls out there who prefer to be kept by their man, but I'm not one of them."

"I know that. Right, here's another solution then. How is your father doing for work now?"

"He's not. Hasn't had any employment except general handyman jobs for months. Why?" She narrowed her eyes inquisitively.

"Hear me out. I've been looking at going down the renovation route, you know, buying rundown houses and selling them for a profit. The one thing that has put me off jumping in is finding a reliable builder who won't rip me off. Do you think your father would be up for that?"

Her eyes widened. "He'd bite your hand off if you suggested that to him. He's really good at his job. You can see for yourself when you visit the house on Sunday. He built the conservatory from scratch himself and maintains the house without Mum ever needing to nag him. Most builders shy away from carrying out work on their own properties. I won't say anything. Why don't you strike up a conversation with him on Sunday about it?" She left her seat, ran around the table, and kissed him on the lips. Then she dashed back and threw herself into her chair again.

"Are you drunk?" he asked, sounding a little taken aback by her exuberant behaviour.

"No, although I would welcome the opportunity after the day I've had."

"Ah, alas, you'd be on your own. I have a PM to perform at seven in the morning. Another urgent case for an impatient Inspector I know."

"We're the pits, aren't we?" She laughed.

"I wouldn't necessarily say that about you, but patience isn't really one of your finer attributes. Not that I'm complaining. You certainly keep me on my toes. That's sorted then, about asking your father. Do you think he'll mind?"

"Not at all, and he definitely won't rip you off. I can't thank you enough for this, Simon."

"Hey, let's wait and see if he agrees first. I've been thinking about property developing for a while now."

"Hey, I think Lorne used to be into property developing. Maybe she can give you a few pointers. I could ask her and Tony, her husband, to come up for the weekend soon to discuss it."

"Of course, I remember her. A very good detective and lovely lady, to boot. That would be amazing. Does she still dabble in it now?"

"No, she runs a rescue centre for abandoned dogs along with her daughter and her husband. He's also a private investigator."

"Crikey! Do they ever get time off?"

"Not much. She's never been the type to sit around and do bugger all on her day off."

"Well, I'd value her opinion, and your father's of course, about a few properties I've had my eye on over the past few weeks."

"How exciting. I'm pretty mean with a paintbrush. I don't mind lending a hand at the end."

"You have enough to do with your own career."

"I know. Oh, well, the option is there if you need it. Dad is going to be thrilled about this. Hey, promise me that you won't take him on just to make me happy."

"I'll guarantee that." He raised his glass and clinked it against hers for the second toast of the evening. "To our new partnership."

"Thank you, Simon. You truly are one in a million. Neither my dad nor I will let you down."

"I love you, Sally Parker."

"I love you, too, Simon Bracknall, expert pathologist and future property developer."

They spent the rest of the evening just enjoying being in each other's company, alone in the restaurant, which anyone would have thought they'd booked for the entire evening. After their meal, they stepped outside to wait for Sally's taxi to arrive. It was drizzling, so Simon insisted that they hang out in his car. Once inside, he leaned over and kissed her. His deep, exploring kiss took her breath away, and because of the drink she had consumed, she felt suddenly light-headed. He reached into the backseat and produced a bunch of red roses. Her eyes filled up with tears.

"Simon, they're beautiful. You shouldn't have."

The taxi's headlights lit up the car as it pulled into the car park alongside them.

"You better go. Thank you for a wonderful evening. I'll call you tomorrow."

Sally kissed him again. "Thank you, for everything. I love you," she slurred, feeling like the luckiest girl in the world.

CHAPTER TWELVE

Sally's head was fuzzy when she woke the following morning amid the bright sunlight flooding her bedroom. She turned over to see the time. It was seven forty-five. "Jesus, I'm going to be late."

She rushed into the bathroom, quickly showered, and ran back into the bedroom, where she slipped into her grey skirt suit and red blouse before drying her hair. She ran down the stairs, let Dex out into the garden, and switched on the kettle. When she looked up at the clock on the wall, she decided she didn't have time for either a drink or breakfast. She wiped Dex's feet and hugged him. "See you later, boy. Behave yourself today." There was no sign of her parents being awake, so she crept out of the house.

It didn't take her long to realise that something was wrong with the car—it was sloping to one side. At first, she thought that her vision was playing tricks on her. However, as she rounded the car, she looked down and saw that both of the nearside tyres had been slashed. She aimed a sharp kick at the deflated rubber. "Damn, damn, damn." Not wanting to go back in the house and wake her parents, she called for a taxi.

She arrived at the station in a foul mood and five minutes later than normal. Jack opened his mouth to say something, and she silenced him with a raised hand. "Don't start on me. Some bastard slashed two of my tyres, and I had to wait for a taxi to pick me up, which took forever because of the roadworks and the mothers dropping their kids off to school. I need a coffee to calm me down."

"Slashed your tyres?" Jack asked, his eyes wide in shock.

"I'm glad there's nothing wrong with your hearing, Jack. Let me go see what rubbish has arrived in the post, and then we'll shoot off." She kicked out at the table leg in front of her. "We've got a bloody lot on today. I could do without this stress first thing in the morning."

"You can't ignore it, boss, not if your tyres were intentionally slashed. We need to look into it."

"I haven't got time, Jack. We'll have to take your car today, sorry."

He shrugged. "It makes no odds to me. But we need to sort out who did that to your car. If I didn't know any better, it looks like someone has a vendetta against you."

"Crap! I never thought about it like that. You're referring to what happened to Dex the other night?"

"Yes. Are your parents aware of this? They should be keeping a vigilant eye open just in case."

"No, they were asleep when I set off. Shit!"

"What?"

"They're always up and about at that time of day. I never thought to check on them or go back in the house to tell them." She pulled her mobile out of her jacket and called home. The phone rang and rang. She was just about to hang up and redial when her father answered the phone, his voice groggy. "Dad, thank God. Are you all right?"

"Sally? Why shouldn't we be? What's wrong, love?"

"I was worried when you didn't answer. Dad, did you see anyone hanging around the house last night?"

"No! What's this about, love?" he asked, sounding more alert.

"I had to ring for a taxi this morning because some arsehole slashed my tyres."

Her dad whistled down the phone, nearly deafening Sally. "What? Outside the house? Last night?"

"Yes, umm... I was tipsy when I came home last night, didn't notice anything wrong. They might have been already damaged. I have no way of knowing."

"Do you want me to sort the tyres out for you, love, or do you think it would be a good idea if you dusted them for prints first?"

"I hadn't thought of that. I'll get onto SOCO right away, see if they can come out this morning. After that, if you wouldn't mind sorting replacements out for me, that would be great. I'll get Jack to drop me home this evening." Sally eyed her partner, who gave her a thumbs-up.

"Any problems, let me know, and I'll come over and pick you up, love. Any ideas who would do such a thing?"

"I'm at a loss right now, Dad. It might have something to do with the case I'm working on. Not sure yet. Keep a watchful eye on things around there, you know, after what happened with Dex the other day..."

"You don't think it could be those skanky bastards who moved out last year?"

"Maybe, but it's been a while. Perhaps they thought they would let the dust settle a little before they took retribution. Let's keep that theory between you and me for now, okay? The last thing we need is Mum's stress levels rocketing again."

"Yes, love. I hear you on that one."

"I'll give you a call back in a sec. Bye for now."

She hung up and rang the Scenes of Crime Department. They agreed to slot a visit in at eleven that morning, in between other jobs they already had booked. Sally called her father back to make him aware of the situation. Then she stopped at the vending machine, grabbed two coffees, and entered her office. The day had only just begun, and she was already exhausted. She looked down at the stack of envelopes littering her desk and threw a bunch of files on them. "I can't handle you yet, boys, sorry."

The shrill of the phone startled her. "Hello. DI Parker. How can I help?"

"Hello, beautiful. I had five minutes spare so thought I'd see how you are?"

"Pissed off and exhausted if you must know," Sally replied, moodily. "I'm sorry, I didn't mean to sound like a grump. Some bugger slashed two of my tyres last night, so the day hasn't started off in the best way."

"That sucks. Any idea when it happened?"

"Nope, I was too tipsy to notice when I got home last night. I'm beginning to think someone has got it in for me."

"Hmm... I have to say the thought crossed my mind, too. Maybe you're getting closer to finding out who the real killer is."

Sally sat upright in her chair. "I wasn't really thinking along those lines, but you could be right. Okay, I better go. Lots to do, people to see, and all that. I'll ring you later on this evening if that's okay, Simon?"

"Of course. I've got a hectic day ahead myself."

Cold Case

Sally hung up, her mood a little brighter after speaking to Simon. *How can I have doubts that he's the right man for me?* She shouldn't was the answer, plain and simple.

Jack knocked on her door and waved his white cotton hanky. "Safe to come in, or am I in danger of getting my head bitten off?"

"Idiot. Sorry for my foul mood. All gone now, thanks to the coffee."

Jack raised an eyebrow. "Really? It never works that quickly for me. Are you sure it wasn't to do with the phone call you just received?"

"Smart arse. Were you spying on me?"

"Nope, wouldn't dream of it. I have better things to do with my day than eavesdrop on a lovers' conversation."

Sally's cheeks felt hot all of a sudden. "Bugger off, Bullet. Are you ready to rumble?" She downed both cool cups of coffee one after the other and walked around the desk towards him.

"I'm ready. It was you holding us up."

"Not anymore. I say we call in to see Dawn Ward first. Let's hope she's in."

They drove out to Thetford, where Parson's Road was a small cul-de-sac separating the edge of town and the wide-open countryside. Sally had always liked this area of Norfolk for that reason. Maybe it was the forest drawing her, although the recent discovery of the two burglars' bodies made her reconsider that idea. The white house had red-painted windowsills and a matching red door and gate. A red Nissan Micra was sitting outside the gate.

"We might be in luck here," Jack announced as they exited the car.

Sally took the lead up the path. The flowerbeds on either side were just showing signs of life. Daffodils waved hello in the breeze, making Sally smile. She was looking forward to the spring and summer ahead. She rang the bell, and within seconds, a blonde woman in her mid-to-late forties, wearing a long jumper over black leggings, opened the door. "Hello, are you Dawn Ward?"

The woman frowned and eyed Sally and Jack nervously. "I am. Who wants to know?"

Sally produced her warrant card and held it up in front of the woman. "DI Sally Parker, and this is my partner, DS Jack Blackman. Would it be possible for us to come inside for a quick chat?"

Mrs. Ward pushed back the door and walked through the house. Jack closed the door behind them. In the kitchen, Mrs. Ward motioned for them to take a seat at a circular pine table. The room was a little cluttered for Sally's taste. Its bookshelves bulged with books, and an untidy pile of toys was stacked in the corner of the room. "Excuse the mess. I look after my grandchild a few days a week."

Sally smiled, hoping to put the woman at ease. "We're here concerning a cold case we're investigating. Maybe you remember the teacher at your son's school who was murdered, Aisha Thomas, the music teacher?"

"I do. Gosh, that was years ago. Are you telling me that her murderer was never found?"

"That's right. Well, some new evidence has come our way recently, hence our need to reinvestigate the case."

"Okay, I'm not sure how I can help, but I'm willing to give it a go."

"We interviewed the teachers in the music department yesterday, and one of them mentioned that you had a run-in with Aisha at one time. Can you tell us in your own words how that incident came about?"

The woman's hand began to shake, and she scratched the side of her face with a painted nail. "I'm not sure I can remember much, really."

"Do your best for us."

"Well, I had a word with her. I suppose you would call it a confrontation. But I soon found out it was all a grave misunderstanding."

"That's interesting. Can you start at the beginning for us?"

"Okay." She sat back in her chair and folded her arms. "I had noticed a change in my son, Daniel, and asked him what was going on, but he refused to tell me. I put two and two together and came up with five. My fault entirely..."

"What do you mean?" Sally asked.

"I forgot that Daniel was having a piano lesson after school one day. I had an appointment and was livid when he wasn't standing at the gates as usual. I spotted one of the music teachers. I think her name was Wall or something like that..."

"Could it have been Ball?"

The woman pointed her finger at Sally. "Yes, that was it. Sorry, it's been a few years. Well, she was in the playground and said that Daniel was having extra tutoring with Mrs. Thomas. There was something in her tone and the way her eyes screwed up that sent the alarm bells ringing in my head. What with the changes I'd seen in Daniel over the months, I went storming in there and slapped Aisha round the face. Seeing them so close together on that piano stool made my blood boil, I can tell you."

"Did you accuse Aisha of anything?"

"Yes, bloody hell, I so regret what I said that day. I've had countless nightmares about it since. I accused her of grooming Daniel. I know it was dreadful of me, but you hear such awful things about what some teachers get up to with their pupils, a red mist descended, and I just couldn't help myself. All I was trying to do was protect my son."

"I can understand that, however, Aisha wasn't guilty of anything other than giving your son extra tutoring."

"I know that now. Daniel went berserk at me when we got home and admitted that he was being bullied by some of the older boys. Since starting his tutoring with Mrs. Thomas, the bullying had subsided. I felt such a fool. I did send Mrs. Thomas a letter of apology, which she gracefully accepted. If that Ball woman hadn't reacted the way she had, I wouldn't have gone storming into the music room like that."

"You think Miss Ball dropped Aisha in it intentionally?"

"I don't know if that's the case or not. I spoke to Lisa about it after Aisha passed away and learned that the two women had never got on. Maybe I just misread the signs and jumped in before I engaged my brain properly. I've felt guilty ever since that day, especially when I heard Aisha had been murdered. It's just awful—the whole damn situation has cursed me to this day."

"By what we know of Aisha, she only had the children's best interests at heart. She wouldn't want you going through life riddled in guilt, I'm sure."

"Thank you. I appreciate your kind words."

"Can you think of any other incidents that happened around that time concerning either Mrs. Thomas or Miss Ball?"

"No, nothing. I kept my head down after my dreadful display. Never really went near the school after that day. I was far too ashamed."

"Okay, then we'll get off. Please try and overcome your guilt. These things happen."

"Not to me, they don't, Inspector. Like I said, a red mist descended that day before I could prevent it."

"There was no real damage done. Thank you for your time." The three of them stood up, and Mrs. Ward led the detectives back to the front door. Sally shook her hand as Jack stepped out.

"Thank you for being so understanding. I hope you catch the person responsible after all these years."

"So do I. Here's my card if you think of anything else we should know about."

"I'll be sure to get in touch. Goodbye." She gently closed the door behind them.

Sally puffed out her cheeks as she walked back to the car. "What a waste of time that was."

"It certainly was. Does this mean we should start pointing the finger at Sandra Ball now?" Jack asked as he dropped into the driver's seat beside her.

"Maybe, maybe not. She might have been guilty of killing Aisha, but what about the two burglars? I doubt she would have known either of them. We've got a connection, remember? We need to treat this case as having three victims and not just the one. My guess is that it'll prevent us taking the wrong route."

"Let's hope we get more luck in seeing Drake."

"We'll call at the school first. I'm not going to bother to ring ahead. He'll have to make time to see us today, or I'll call him into the station to be interviewed."

Jack drove the short route to the school. They entered the building and headed down the winding corridors to the music rooms. Pamela Albright was just coming out of one of the rooms as they turned the final corner. "Hello again. Back so soon?"

Sally smiled. "We were hoping to have a quick word with Jonathon Drake if that's all right, just so we can wrap up this part of the investigation today."

"I see. Well, I have to tell you that he rang in sick this morning. Had a bad reaction to something the dentist gave him yesterday during his treatment. Never heard anything like that before, I must say. Do you think it's a man thing?"

Sally turned to face Jack and raised an eyebrow.

"Hey, don't look at me. There's a reason I avoid going to the dentist."

Sally's eyes rolled up to the ceiling. He'd totally misread her expression. Ignoring her partner, she faced Mrs. Albright again. "That's very strange. Even when I had my wisdom teeth out a few years back, I was still at work the next day. Men are such babies. No problem, we've got his address. We'll call round and see him. Please don't contact him with our intentions."

"I'm far too busy around here reorganising Jonathon's classes to be concerned about ringing him. Let me know if he's not at home, if you would, and I'll throw the book at him for playing truant."

Sally laughed. "Will you put him in detention?"

Mrs. Albright's stern face cracked, then she winked and said, "I might be tempted to cane him. Not sure detention acts as much of a deterrent nowadays."

Sally and Jack left the school and raced over to Jonathon Drake's address. "Let's see what he has to say for himself. Looks like it's the second-floor flat we're after."

Sally rang the bell. She heard it chime on the other side of the door, but no one answered. She stepped back and looked up. "Hmm... unless my focus is still a little fuzzy from the wine I consumed last night, I'd swear I've just seen the curtain twitch."

Jack joined her and surveyed the upstairs front window for himself. "Nah, you must have been imagining it."

Sally wasn't so sure, though. She opened the letterbox and shouted, "Mr. Drake, it's the police. We'd like a little chat if we could, sir. We know you're in there. Please open the door."

Jack had remained looking up at the upstairs window. He shook his head when Sally turned to face him. "Nothing, boss."

She lowered her voice and said, "Well, that's strange. I'm just not prepared to throw in the towel just yet. I believe he's up there. You stay here while I knock on the neighbours' doors." She rang the bell to the lower flat, but that also went unanswered. So she walked back down the path and into the house over to the right. She banged the front door's knocker, and it was immediately opened by a grey-haired man who walked with a frame. "Hello, sir. I'm sorry to disturb you, but I was wondering if you've seen your neighbour today."

"No, Doris is away a lot, helping out at her daughter's house. She's just had a little nipper, you see."

"That's nice. I was talking about the gentleman in the flat above, Jonathon Drake?"

"Silly me. Who are you, first? From the council?"

"No, I'm a detective with the Norfolk Constabulary." Sally showed him her ID.

"Oh, dear... in a spot of bother, is he?"

"Not as far as we know. We just need to question him about something. Have you seen him today?"

"He went out yesterday, he's a teacher. I noticed he came home later than normal. If I didn't know any better, I'd say he was in a bit of pain, holding the side of his face he was."

"Maybe he had a trip to the dentist."

"Yes, you could be right. Anyway, he seemed all right when he left for work this morning. I was very surprised to see him come back about twenty minutes later. I thought he'd forgotten something, but he never appeared again."

"So you think he might still be in there?" Sally's suspicions escalated to high alert.

"I can't be a hundred percent sure on that, dear. I have a weak bladder and have to take frequent trips to the loo, but I don't remember seeing him come out again. I sit in there all day, like to watch the world go by rather than be glued to the damn telly and that god-awful daytime TV."

"That's very interesting. I thought I saw the curtain twitch, but I wasn't sure. I'll try again. Thank you for your help, sir."

"Anytime, dear. Always happy to help the police in their duties."

Sally waved at the man from the gate and proceeded to try the neighbour on the other side to see if they could corroborate the other neighbour's story. A woman wearing a pink flowery apron opened the door. She swept back the grey hair that had flopped across her eyes and smiled at Sally. "Can I help? Excuse the mess. I'm in the middle of baking cakes for the Women's Institute."

"Sorry to disrupt your creativity. I was wondering if you've seen your neighbour today. Jonathon Drake, in the upstairs flat."

The woman's forehead creased. "Are you sure you have the right flat or the right name? I thought it was something different to that. Let me think... I had a letter for him the other week that was put through my door by mistake. Bloomin' heck, what is wrong with my bloody memory? Wait, it's coming... Paul something."

Sally's heart skipped several beats. "There's no rush, in your own time."

"I knew it would come to mind eventually. Paul Marwood."

"Are you sure?"

"Yes, dear. Now that I've remembered, there's no mistaking it. I saw the letter addressed to him with my own eyes. I knocked on the door and gave it to him personally. Thought he would be pleased, but he snatched it from my hand and slammed the door in my face. Didn't even say thank you for my trouble. I've not given him the time of day since. If I get another letter for him, I'll put 'return to sender, unknown at this address' next time. Ungrateful so-and-so."

"You've been very helpful. One last thing... he couldn't have another person staying at the flat with him?"

Her mouth twisted from side to side. "I never thought of that. I wouldn't like to say, love. The thing is, these are only one-bedroom flats."

"Again, thanks for your help. I hope I haven't disrupted your baking for too long."

"Happy to oblige. I'm sure my Victoria sponges will survive."

Sally motioned for Jack to join her. She didn't want to let Drake know what she had to say if he was eavesdropping on the other side of the door.

"What is it, boss?"

"Drake might well be going under a different name. I think we should get back in the car and drive off. We'll double back in a few minutes, see if Drake is tempted to leave the house. He's not likely to do that if he spots us sitting in the car outside his flat."

"Good idea. Maybe we should contact the station, see if Joanna can work her magic and come up with the goods on the new name we have for the bugger."

"You read my mind, Jack. You drive while I call Joanna."

Jack pulled away from the kerb and parked in the pub car park at the end of the road, where they had a good view of Drake's front door.

Sally rang the station. "Joanna, I need you to drop what you're doing and run a name for me—a Paul Marwood. We believe Drake might be using an assumed name."

"I see. Running it through the system now."

Sally looked over her shoulder at Drake's flat while she listened to Joanna pounding away on her keyboard. "Whoa! You're never gonna believe this, boss."

Sally sighed. "Hit me with it."

"Paul Marwood was banged up for a sexual assault on a minor. I couldn't find him on the sex offender list probably because of when the incident happened."

"What the fuck? How many times are we going to hear this? On the sex offender list or not he shouldn't be working in a school. Don't these bloody schools do their background checks properly? Right, get me a warrant for his arrest and another to search his home address, pronto, Joanna. I will not have filth like him walking the streets on my patch. Get me the number of his probation officer, too. When was he in prison?"

"I'll action it right away, boss. I totally agree with you. He got out of prison over twelve years ago. Do you think he would still be under a probation officer?"

"Bugger, probably not, but he must have been under one at the time he started at the school, right?"

"I'll get the warrants sorted first and get back to you with the probation officer's name ASAP."

Sally prodded the end-call button. "Assault on a minor, he got out of prison twelve years ago."

"I doubt the offender list was in action back then, boss. That shouldn't make a difference though, he would have got out under a probation officer. How many times do we stumble across things like this?" Jack said, sounding equally angry about the news. "Hold on. I think that's him."

Jack started the car and circled the car park, then he raced back to Drake's flat and screeched to a halt. Sally and Jack both jumped out of the car and chased after the man. He was tall and lanky, and the way he took off gave Sally the feeling that he looked after himself and was probably used to jogging. Sally was already beginning to tire. "Don't lose him, Jack. Keep on him. I'll go back for the car."

"Jesus, thanks, boss. I'll do my best, but I fear he's going to get away from us."

Drake ran down a narrow road, out of sight, as Sally began jogging back to the car. She caught up with her partner within a few seconds and flung open the passenger door. "Get in. We'll try and cut him off."

"The trouble is he knows the blasted area better than us. Hey, boss, easy as you go with my car," he pleaded as Sally crunched through the gears in the unfamiliar car.

"Don't worry. I won't damage your precious car. I forgot how possessive you men can be."

"Er, if you don't mind, I'd rather you stop talking and concentrate on your driving."

Sally patted his knee. "Don't fret."

Jack gripped her hand and placed it back on the steering wheel. She rounded the next corner and spotted Drake again. Putting her foot down, she pulled up close behind him, only for him to dip down another alley. Sally braked and reversed. "Shit, I was hoping it was a dead end."

"No such luck. Keep driving—we should meet up with him in the next street."

Sally pressed down hard on the accelerator, but when she turned into the next road, there was no sign of Drake. "Damn! He must have doubled back. I'll turn around and go after him." She proceeded to do an expert three-point turn in the road. Halfway through, she looked over at Jack, whose eyes were shut tight. "Oh ye of little faith, you can look now."

Jack exhaled a large breath. "Nice job. Waste of time, though, boss. He's nowhere to be seen."

Sally slapped the steering wheel. "Where is he? He must be around here somewhere." They cruised the area for the next ten minutes, but it was a waste of time.

"Maybe we should swap over," Jack suggested.

Sally's phone rang, and they quickly switched places before she answered the call. "Hi, Joanna. What news do you have?"

"I've got the number for the probation officer, boss. She's expecting your call." Joanna reeled off the number, and Sally noted it down in her notebook.

"That's brilliant. We're still on the look-out for Drake; he outran us. Put out an alert for him, will you? Even if it's with the old photo you have of him."

"Will do, boss."

Sally hung up and rang the probation service. "Miss Anderson?"

"It is. Who's calling?"

"My name is DI Sally Parker. One of my colleagues just rang you."

"Ah, yes. How can I help, Inspector?"

"Paul Marwood. I wondered if you could fill in a few gaps for me."

"I'll do my best. Let me locate his file. It's been a few years since I've had any contact with him."

Sally waited patiently for a few moments before the woman came back on the line.

"Here we are. He was under my care for two years after coming out of prison. After that, he was free to live his life."

"What about the sex offender list? Wouldn't that affect his probation record?"

"The sex offender list is a relatively new thing, Inspector. Anyone serving time before it came in wouldn't have been put on the list."

"So before it became law, these people were under your authority and then just let loose on the community again? Is that what you're telling me?"

"It was how things happened in those days, Inspector. Things are a lot tighter nowadays."

"Are they? So, maybe you can tell me how a man who has served time in prison for sexual assault is allowed to get a job as a music teacher in a secondary school in the area?"

The woman gasped. "He what? I had no idea."

"It's not the first time we've heard something like this occurring. Why is the system breaking down like this, Miss Anderson?"

"I haven't got a clue. His name should have been recognised when anyone tapped into the system to check his background information."

"I know he's now going under a different name. Do you people realise how easy it is to obtain another identity?"

"We're obviously not aware. Otherwise, this type of situation wouldn't occur. We're not at fault here, Inspector."

"No, I know—the system is. But someone has to look out for our children. Maybe you should pass that on to your bosses, Miss Anderson. Because when the system fails, it's up to us to pick up the goddamn pieces."

"Will that be all, Inspector? I have a meeting to attend," the woman asked curtly.

"Yes, for now. I'll let you know if we find out if Marwood—or Drake, as he's known now—has either molested a child or killed one of the other teachers at the school, because that is what this phone call is about. He's just become a prime suspect in a murder enquiry."

Sally ended the call before the woman could reply. She glared at the phone. "Stick that in your bloody pipe and smoke it... agh! Some people really do get on my tits. Her I'm-only-doing-my-job attitude stinks. Let's get back to the station, Jack."

"It would be pointless telling you to calm down, I suppose?"

"Yep, I'm seething. Makes you wonder if anyone takes pride in their jobs anymore, or if they just turn up for the pay packet at the end of the month."

"I take it you're not referring to us when you say that?"

"Definitely not, partner," she declared, shaking her head in despair.

CHAPTER THIRTEEN

Jack opened the door to the station's entrance just as two uniformed officers were leaving the building. They seemed jovial, laughing at something, and were oblivious to those around them until Sally spoke.

"Hello, Patrick. How are you doing?"

Patrick Thomas's face dropped. "Hello, Inspector. I'm coping as well as can be expected. Any news on the case yet? I was going to contact you later to see how things are going." He shuffled his feet uncomfortably as his partner stepped away from the conversation.

"Saved you a job then, haven't I? The case is progressing slowly. Actually, I'm glad I've bumped into you, because I wanted to ask you a personal question."

"Fire away, Inspector."

"I need to ask you if either you or your wife had money troubles around the time of her death."

His gaze drifted out to the car park as he thought, then returned to her. "Yes, we did... well, not exactly money troubles, but we did take out a dubious loan. Aisha was desperate to have a child, so we borrowed five thousand pounds for fertility treatment."

"Dubious loan? Care to expand on that?"

"I was furious when Aisha told me what she'd done. I came home from work one day and found a wad of money fanned out on the kitchen table. When I asked her where she'd got the money from, she told me she'd contacted someone through an advert in the local paper. I was livid. Told her to return the money immediately as I thought it was from a loan shark. I was right. She was adamant that she wasn't going to return it. I remember we didn't speak for a few days. She didn't have a clue about things like that. No idea the damage these people can do if you don't keep up the exorbitant payments. She refused to listen to me because she was so desperate to have a child." He turned to look at his partner. "You remember that, don't you, Caroline?"

Caroline's gaze sharply went from Patrick to Sally and back to Patrick again. "Gosh, I had totally forgotten all about that, Pat. Awful situation, I seem to recall."

"Can you remember the name of this loan shark?"

He tutted as if annoyed at himself. "Spike someone... can't for the life of me think of his surname."

"Does Spike Barker ring a bell?" Sally enquired.

He nodded. "Yes, that's it."

"Can I ask what happened to the money you borrowed?"

"Aisha insisted we use it for what it was intended for. We had a course of fertility treatment booked. The first appointment was to have been the week after her death," he replied sadly.

"I'm sorry to hear that. What happened regarding the payments to the loan shark?"

"I ended up borrowing the money off a friend. I'd rather be in debt to a friend than one of those thieving shits. I turned up to repay the money, and even though we'd only had the loan a month or so, he wanted an extra grand on top. That's how these scumbags work. Once you're in their grasp, they tighten the bloody vise and keep tightening it around your balls whether you want to pay the debt off early or not."

"Didn't you try to report him?"

"I had a word with my sergeant, but he said it was futile going over to see Barker, as he ran a 'legitimate business'."

"I'm sorry about that. So where did you find the extra thousand to pay him off?"

Patrick's gaze dropped to the ground. "From another friend."

"Okay, that's really useful information. Thanks. I'll let you both get on with your work now. I'll be in touch soon if I have any news for you."

Jack and Sally watched the two officers walk away before they entered the station.

"What are you thinking?" Jack asked as they walked up the stairs.

"The wife takes on a debt that neither of them can afford, and a few weeks later, she's found murdered?"

"Are you pointing the finger at *him*?"

Sally shook her head. "Oh, I don't know, Jack. We need to find out more about this loan shark. That's got to be our next move. Let's see what the others have come up with and go through the facts again."

"What about Drake?"

"There's an alert gone out for his arrest. Once we get the warrant, we can go back there and search the place. Would a child molester turn around and kill an adult?"

"Well, he's on the run for a reason. Maybe Aisha got in his way. Maybe he had his eye on one of the pupils and Aisha confronted him about it."

"We have a lot of speculation brewing but no concrete evidence to back anything up—that's what is so bloody annoying about this case."

They walked into the incident room, and Sally headed towards Joanna's desk while Jack grabbed a couple of coffees from the machine. He deposited Sally's beside her on the desk as Joanna went through what she'd come up with regarding the loan shark.

"He was banged up six years ago, boss. Was found guilty of GBH, beat up several people who refused to pay back some of their loans. He got out of prison in July last year. As far as I can see, he's kept his nose clean since then."

Sally frowned. "He hasn't gone back to running his distasteful business? That seems odd."

Joanna shrugged. "He has a wife. Maybe he's put the business in her name. I'll look into it, see what I can find."

"Good idea. Give me ten minutes in my office, and then we'll go through what we've got so far. Any news on the warrants?"

"I've stated the urgency behind the request, boss, but nothing has materialised as yet."

"Okay, I'll leave it until mid-afternoon and chase them up myself."

Sally drifted into the office with her cup of coffee and stopped to gaze out the window for a second or two. Bathed in the sun's rays, she contemplated why they weren't more advanced in the case. She finished her coffee, ignored the post on her desk, and returned to the incident room.

She drew everyone's attention to the whiteboard she was standing next to. "Let's thrash this out. I want to hear what you think about each suspect on the list. Don't hold back. We're missing a vital clue somewhere, and we need to locate that clue. Otherwise, this case will end up defeating us. I'm not about to let that happen."

Sally turned to the board, picked up the marker pen sitting on the shelf, and added to the list of suspects on the left-hand side. "On the run, we have Jonathon Drake a.k.a. Paul Marwood. Not suspected of anything other than working illegally with children so far—if that's the case, then why is he on the run? Jack came up with the idea that maybe he was getting close to a child and possibly Aisha either confronted him with her suspicions or threatened to report him. Would that really cause him to go after Aisha and kill her? If so, where's the connection with the two burglars? We mustn't forget that part of the equation in all this. I think that is going to be the crucial piece of the puzzle."

Joanna tapped her pen against her cheek. "Maybe once we get hold of the search warrant, something will show up in his flat that will highlight a connection, boss. Perhaps he was friends with the burglars. Maybe their paths crossed while they were in prison. I'll have to check out the dates."

"Okay, I'm going to point you in the direction of a dubious lead in the shape of Sandra Ball, music teacher at Highfield School. According to another music teacher, there was no love lost between the women. I honestly don't think it's anything more than a case of jealousy, but I'd like to keep her in mind anyway. She's also guilty of stirring up trouble with one of the parents, and that led to Aisha being struck around the face by this lady, Dawn Ward." Sally circled the name on the board. "We need to look into her background, not that I think much will show up. After talking to her this morning, I believe she was wound up by Sandra Ball and went on to accuse Aisha of trying to groom her son. Sounds like bullshit to me. I don't believe for one minute Aisha could have been like that, but it's not something we should discount, either."

Jordan raised his hand to speak. "If—and it's a big if—she was grooming this boy, maybe that's a link we should be looking into with Drake."

"Another good idea. Well done, Jordan. We'll bear it in mind when we search Drake's address. We've also got Warren Dean, who, to me, is another prime suspect in this case. Aisha's neighbour has suggested that he's a bigoted racist who was constantly badgering Aisha. Again, we have to ask ourselves where the connection between him and the other two victims is. Maybe he knew the burglars. Hard to say without interviewing him, which isn't likely to happen any time soon."

"That's the frustrating part about this guy." Stuart sat forward in his chair. "Would it be worth getting in touch with the German police about questioning him?"

"That's a great idea, Stuart, however, if he knows we're onto him, he might go on the run in Germany. He's due back in the country in a few weeks. We'll have to be patient until we can haul his arse in. One other thing: Jack and I bumped into Patrick Thomas as we returned to the station. Given what we've learnt about the two burglars, Wilson and Jenkinson, and their money troubles, I asked him if either he or Aisha had any debts at the time of her death. He told us that Aisha had gone to a loan shark for a five-thousand-pound loan to enable her to have fertility treatment. The loan shark was none other than Spike Barker."

"Hence you wanting to know what he was up to?" Joanna asked.

"Yes, that's right. That's going to be my next stop, if you can get me his address, Joanna, please?"

Joanna left her seat and rushed to her desk. She scribbled down an address and handed it to Sally.

"Brilliant. So, does anyone else have anything they'd like to highlight?"

"What about the husband, boss?" Stuart asked. "Is he in the clear?"

"Not at this moment, Stuart. I've still got him high on the list, but with no incriminating evidence pointing his way. This loan debacle has highlighted him again, however. We'll know more after we've interviewed the loan shark. Again, where would the connection be with the burglars?"

Jack cleared his throat, ready to speak. "Perhaps he was already aware of the burglars. He's a copper after all."

"That's true and a very plausible link. Well done, partner. Right, you guys get some lunch. Jack and I will have ours on the way to see Barker. Keep digging and do what you do best. I'm proud of what we've achieved thus far this week. Keep up the good work."

The team got back to work. Jack and Sally left the incident room and made their way over to Barker's address.

En route, Sally's mobile rang. "Hi, Joanna, what have you got for us?"

"I wanted to catch you before you began questioning Barker, boss. I've looked into any business dealings that might be in his wife's name and—bingo! I found a loan company called Midas Loans registered to their home address."

"Bloody marvellous! Well done, Joanna. We've just arrived, so excellent timing on your part." She ended the call and smiled at Jack. "A leopard never changes its spots. How stupid do these idiots think we are?"

Jack laughed and shook his head. "He'd have to be smarter than that to get one over on you, boss."

"Let's see what the little shit has to say for himself, shall we?"

The house was a huge Georgian manor with a large gravelled drive at the front. Sally rang the ornate doorbell, and the tone echoed inside the house for a few seconds before the door opened.

A smartly dressed blonde woman chewing gum leant against the doorframe. "Yeah, what do you want? You look like the filth to me."

"Who is it, Marissa?" a man's voice asked from a distant room behind her.

Sally and Jack produced their warrant cards.

More chewing ensued, then the woman replied, "See, I can smell you lot from ten miles away."

"You're very astute, Mrs. Barker. May we come in?"

"What for?"

A scrawny-looking man in his early forties appeared behind the woman and mumbled something incoherent under his breath. "What do you lot want? I'm straight now, have been for years."

"Because of your enforced imprisonment, I suppose," Sally replied with a beaming smile. "We'd just like a brief chat. We can either do it here or down at the station—the choice is yours."

The man walked away from them and called over his shoulder, "You better let them in, love, or they'll only invent another charge to put me away again."

"You can come in for ten minutes maximum. I have an appointment to keep at the hairdresser's, and I want you out of my house by then. I ain't leaving you alone with my Spike. Not after last time. Ended up with a busted nose and two crushed fingers because of your bloody lot."

Sally grinned at the woman. There was no way on earth she was about to apologise to the likes of them for another colleague's behaviour.

Sally and Jack walked through the large, well-lit hallway, which was dominated by a curved glass staircase, and into an expansive lounge at the rear of the property. It overlooked a pool area immediately outside the bi-fold doors, which were open to the beautiful landscaped garden beyond. Sally's envy gene was on high alert. The place was magnificent, but it stuck in her gut that all Barker's money had been obtained from desperate people.

The furniture was in soft muted tones, and there were plenty of gilded elements to the room in the shape of ornate picture frames and a huge mirror in a gold-plated frame hung above the marble fireplace.

"Do you mind if we sit down?" Sally asked.

"No, I'm not having your stench on my furniture. Outside on the patio. Spike can hose that down once you've gone," Mrs. Barker screeched, much to her husband's amusement.

"You might want to watch your mouth," Jack warned the woman.

"I'll do and say what I like in my own home. We could always do this outside on the drive if you'd rather?" Mrs. Barker snapped at him.

Sally placed her hand on Jack's arm. "It's all right, Jack. On the patio would be fine. It's too stuffy in here for me."

Marissa Barker glared at Sally. "What do you mean by that?"

Sally smiled broadly and shrugged. "It's a warm day."

The four of them went outside onto the patio. Before Sally and Jack could sit down, Marissa swiped the cushions off the seats, leaving them to sit on the uncomfortable wicker. *You really are an insufferable bitch. Any thoughts of this being a nice, friendly interview have gone out the window now, lady, and it's all your fault.* "Take notes if you will, Jack, thanks."

Jack opened his notebook, his pen poised.

Marissa sat next to her husband. She grasped his hand and held it on the glass-topped table. "What can I do for you, Inspector? A warning if I may: if your questions get too invasive, I'll be forced to put a halt to this interview and call my solicitor," Spike said.

"Fine. I have no objections to your solicitor being here from the start if you think you have something to hide. Like I said, this will be an informal chat." *Damn, that's put paid to my idea of coming down heavy on the bastard.*

"Nah, you're all right for now, just warning you." Spike turned to smile at his wife, then he raised her hand and kissed it. Marissa wriggled in her seat and giggled like a teenager.

Sally felt sick at the overly exuberant display of affection. Hearing Jack sigh heavily, she almost burst into laughter. Instead, she cleared her throat and asked, "I need you to cast your mind back to ten years ago, Mr. Barker."

"You can call me Spike. Mr. Barker sounds too toffee-nosed for this time of day."

"Thanks, Spike it is. Ten years ago, you were deep into your loan-sharking business, I believe."

"Wrong. I had a legitimate loan business. It's the filth who labelled me a loan shark."

"Okay, whatever the term you wish to use. What was the aim of that business?"

"Are you bloody serious? It was a loan company. We dished out loans to people," he replied, a large dose of sarcasm thrown into the mix.

"And who did you offer these loans to? Businesses?"

He roared with laughter. "You really are a dumb broad, ain't ya?"

His wife chuckled.

Sally threw Jack a warning glance and nudged his leg under the table to keep calm. "It's a simple question. I'm just trying to get a feel for your company and the service you provided back then."

"My clientele were those in need who had been refused a loan from the bank."

"That was very charitable of you. Did you have many clients? Or would you call them 'customers'?"

"I used to call them something else entirely, but that name is not for ladies' ears." He laughed again.

The more he laughed, the more Sally detested the man and what he stood for. He'd probably spent half his adult life laughing at other people's unfortunate circumstances. People like him deserved to be dropped on a desert island somewhere and left for the wildlife to feed off their bones. "So you helped the needy and the vulnerable. Is that correct?"

"Yeah, if you like. We've already established that. So what? Why are you here, badgering me like this?"

"Badgering you? I'd hardly class a few questions as badgering you. Okay, here's where this is leading. You issued these loans with high interest rates. Is that right?"

"Yes, why shouldn't I? I was willing to fork out the money when the crappy banks turned their backs on these people."

"Bear with me—and what would happen if people didn't repay the loans?"

"I never had anyone who didn't repay what was due."

Sally raised her eyebrow at him. "Seriously? No one ever backed out of their agreement with you? I find that hard to believe. Or are you telling me that the loan came with an ultimatum attached?"

He shrugged. "It might have done."

"Would you mind telling me how that ultimatum was worded? Just for our records."

"What's the point? I ain't in the trade now. Why the bloody hell are you bothered about what went on ten years ago anyway?"

"I'll get to that in a moment. I need to find out how your business worked first. Say I took out a loan and couldn't meet the payments, what would happen to me?"

"I'd send a couple of my boys around to issue a friendly reminder that the payment was due."

"And supposing I'd had a run of bad luck and simply didn't have a couple of pounds to go towards the loan repayment, what would your boys do then?"

"Take a few of your possessions. You would be able to buy the possessions back at a later date."

"On top of the missed loan repayment not instead of it, right?"

He tapped his nose and winked at her. "You've got the drift. Clever, ain't ya?"

"I try my best. So, that's one scenario covered. What would your boys do in the event that the person didn't have any possessions to barter with?"

Spike's eyes narrowed. "Is this some kind of trick question?"

"No, I'm genuinely interested. I'll tell you why in a second."

"My boys would rough the person up a little."

"Now we're getting somewhere. And in the likelihood that person would fail to meet a payment the second time, how would they be treated then?"

"You're taking the piss now, love. I don't have to answer that."

Sally glanced at Jack, who had looked up from his notebook and was giving Spike the evil eye.

"Answer the Inspector's question or we'll haul your arse down the station, got that, buddy?"

Spike bristled under Jack's glare, intimidated by his tone and his threat. "My boys have been known to go a bit too far on occasion."

"Are we talking about putting punters in hospital, or worse than that?"

Spike's gaze surveyed his surroundings, and a large sigh escaped his lips. "I don't believe you haven't looked back on your records about this."

"The case we're working on hasn't allowed me to do that as yet. Why don't you save me the time and tell me what route that kind of negligence might take?"

"Two of my men got a little carried away and ended up killing a punter. That's why I was put in the nick."

"For manslaughter or murder?"

"Neither. My brief got me off on a lesser charge. Those guys went against my wishes and paid the price."

"They went to prison on a murder charge then, yes?"

"Yeah, they deserved that."

"Who was the unfortunate punter who lost his life?"

He shrugged. "I can't remember the name. Some waster who enjoyed the poker tables too much. His stakes got too high, and his gambling debts got out of control—twenty grand, on top of what he owed me. He had no intention of repaying my dosh, so the boys went over there to teach him a lesson. They got carried away, had no idea this guy had a weak heart, and he ended up having a heart attack. They barely touched him."

"That's very unfortunate. Is there ever a time when you refuse to give people a loan?"

Spike thought over her question for a second or two then replied, "No, because everyone signs the agreement to pay back that loan, even if it takes years."

"Which is why you charge the extortionate interest rates?"

"I have to make money somehow. Will you get to the point of this visit? All these facts could have been found online. Ever heard of Google?"

Sally wanted to swipe the smug grin off his face. "Do the names Wilson and Jenkinson ring a bell?"

He ran a hand through his thinning spiky hair. "Should they?"

"Think back to around ten years ago, maybe a little before that, possibly eleven. They both came to you for a loan."

"And what about them? Nothing is registering with me so far. Why should I remember their names in particular?"

"Because they both went missing around the time they owed you money. We've been told by their respective partners that you went after them to recover your debt."

"Jesus, I'm with you now. They were two scallies who my guys found out were burgling the community—is that the ones?"

"Yes, so you just gave up on the men and turned your attention to their womenfolk instead?"

"Yeah, that's the way it works. In my book, the whole family is responsible for that debt. Can you imagine how many fuckers take the money and run? Dozens! The agreement they sign states that the debt belongs to the household and isn't just a personal debt to the one taking out the loan."

"Really? And the punters are aware of that clause when they sign the contract, or is it buried deep in the small print?"

"It's up to them to read the small print before adding their moniker to the paperwork."

"That's appalling and surely wouldn't stand up in a court of law."

"A lot you know then, because it was my bloody solicitor who drew up the agreement, and he's as straight as they come."

I doubt that, buster, but I'll be sure to check into that. "When Wilson and Jenkinson absconded, did you try and find them?"

"I did. My guys searched for the little shits for weeks when their wives said they'd done a bunk."

"Here's my dilemma. How do I know that you didn't put the frighteners on them before they were reported missing?"

"What the fuck are you saying?"

"New evidence has been uncovered this week... when I say 'uncovered', what I'm really saying is that we discovered the bodies of Wilson and Jenkinson buried in a shallow grave on the edge of Thetford Forest."

Spike pushed back his chair and paced the patio before he pointed a wagging finger at Sally. "No frigging way are you pinning that shit on me. I ain't going down for another couple of murders. No way!"

"Calm down, Mr. Barker. Take a seat." His genuine reaction told Sally that he probably hadn't directly had anything to do with the burglars' deaths, but that didn't mean his boys hadn't. "What about your boys? Could they have carried out the deed and not told you?"

"No way. My boys are loyal. They would've told me."

"Okay, that aside, I have another line of questions to ask you regarding an incident that occurred around that time."

"What is this? You've uncovered a few murders, and you thought you'd try to pin them all on me just because I've got a record?"

"No, it's not that at all. Hear me out first. Do you recall authorising a loan to an Aisha Thomas?"

He clawed at his temple as if the inside of his head itched. "I can't remember, and that's the truth."

"Maybe her husband's name will help you remember? Patrick Thomas."

"Vaguely. Why?"

"You must have read about the case or heard her name mentioned on the news at the time."

"Who has time to watch the news? I know I didn't in those days."

"She was found murdered in her home, not long after she returned from her job as a music teacher at Highfield School. Ringing any bells now?"

"Nope, still nothing concrete."

"She was married to a police officer. How about that?"

"Now I've got you."

"Her death was never solved, so we're working on the cold case at present."

"And? What's this got to do with you coming here today?" His brow furrowed, and his lip curled up at one side as he glared at her.

"During our investigation, we found a tenuous link between Aisha Thomas, Wilson and Jenkinson—all three murder victims whom we've spent the last fifteen minutes discussing."

"Get on with it, Inspector. You're talking in bloody riddles."

"That link, Mr. Barker, leads back to you and your business. Now do you see where this line of questioning is going?"

"No way! You can't pin anything on me, lady. No frigging way! The bitch wanted the money to make a sprog with her old man through IVF. I lent her the money so her dream could come true. No way did I go round there and frigging kill her after I'd given her the dosh, if that's what you're implying."

"Ah, so you do remember the woman in question, after all?"

"Yeah, it suddenly came to me. I'll tell you this, though. When the hubby came to pay off the debt, I was surprised he'd taken up with that bird so soon after his beloved wife had departed."

Sally shot Jack a puzzled look then turned back to Barker. "He turned up to see you with a lady friend?"

"Hey, she looked more than just a friend to me, lady, if you get my drift."

"Can you describe this woman?"

"It's been ten years, for fuck's sake."

"Please try. It could be the break we're looking for." Sally offered him a strained smile.

"Don't quote me on this, but she was about his height. Either brown or red hair—can't really remember, but it definitely wasn't blonde." He faced his wife and pecked her on the cheek. "I'm partial to blondes, so I would have definitely remembered that."

"Brilliant. I don't suppose you heard him use her name?"

"Nah, that's as good as the memory gets, sorry."

"That'll do for now then, unless you would consider working with a police sketch artist to help us ascertain her identity."

"Nah, it wouldn't work. I couldn't give the artist any more than I've given you already."

"That is a shame."

"So, does this mean that I'm off the hook now? Are you going to start pointing the finger in the husband's direction?"

"It means we have another line of enquiry open to us. If we arrest someone, would you be willing to come in for a line-up?"

"Me on the other side of a line-up—that's bloody comical, that is! Yeah, if that's what it will take to keep you lot off my back, then count me in."

Sally slid one of her cards across the table. "See, that was pretty harmless, wasn't it? If you think of anything else after we leave, please get in touch straight away, day or night."

"Yep, will do."

Mrs. Barker was the first to stand, followed by Sally and Jack. "I'll show you out."

"We really appreciate your time and help, thanks," Sally said as she passed Barker, who was about to light up the largest Cuban cigar she'd ever seen.

"Don't make a habit of turning up at my door, Inspector. I've gone straight now."

"Maybe you shouldn't have set up another loan business in your wife's name, since that's what led us to your door in the first place." Sally winked and walked back into the lounge.

Marissa slammed the front door behind them, almost catching Jack on the backside. "Bloody cheek. Are you sure we can't pin something on the bastard, just to teach them both another lesson?"

Sally laughed. "Let's get back to the station."

Once they'd returned, Sally brought the team together to share the news they had gathered.

"Whoa, boss, are you saying this means that Patrick Thomas is our main suspect now?" Joanna asked, flabbergasted.

"It's going to be hard to discount him. Let's keep digging for now. We've still got two suspects that we haven't spoken to as yet."

"Are we going to question the husband again?" Jack asked.

"I need more facts first, not forgetting we have this other woman that we should start looking into. Didn't Patrick say that he hadn't been with anyone since his wife's death, Jack?"

"That's right. His partner said he was an only child, maybe he's got a sister that she didn't know about? On the other hand, I suppose it could have been Caroline he was talking about. Maybe he showed up there with his partner while they were on duty one day."

"Let's look into his family members, perhaps he didn't have a sister but a cousin he was close to. Anything else show up while we were out?" The team responded with a mixture of shrugs and the shaking of heads. "That's not good. I really don't want us to pin all our hopes on one person only to find that person innocent, like the original investigation."

Sally walked into her office and rang Simon. "Hi, it's me again."

"Hello, Me Again. You just caught me having a coffee and catching up on some paperwork before my next PM. How's it going?"

"The case? It isn't, not really. I've got a list of suspects, so I suppose we're one up on the original team, but nothing that would hold up in court. We've got a suspect on the run, plus one who is presently out of the country. Once we question them, we should be a step nearer to cracking the case. Our hands are tied now, though, and it's just so frustrating. We did learn that the husband had a girlfriend, according to the loan shark we questioned earlier today, but he could have made a mistake. We're checking to see if Patrick has any female relatives around his age. According to his partner she thought he was an only child, or we're thinking he might have shown up there with his partner, perhaps after their shift had ended one day."

"Very interesting. Can you trust what this loan shark says?"

"It's a case of having to at this point, but yes, we're being cautious. That's why I have refrained from calling him in for another interview."

"I see. Maybe we should see if the bite mark on Aisha's arm matches the husband."

"Hmm... perhaps we should leave that for now. Let's see what the search for relatives comes up with first, and then I can come back to that. Any news at your end, regarding any links to other murders found in the area at the time?"

"No, nothing. I heard about half an hour ago, sorry."

"Never mind. It was worth a shot. I think I'm going to call it a day soon. Can't wait to see you on Sunday. Don't go bringing any fancy bottles of wine with you. Remember my folks are simple people."

"Thanks for the warning. Maybe it is a little early to bring out the champagne, especially as you haven't given me your answer yet."

Sally groaned. "Please don't keep heaping the pressure on me. I'm still mulling things over, but I promise to give you an answer soon. Let's see how you get on with my parents first."

"Is that what this boils down to? Whether or not I get on with your parents?"

"No, I didn't necessarily mean it like that. I wish you'd stop twisting my words. I'm going to hang up before one of us says the wrong thing."

"Coward!"

"Yep, I'll give you a ring tomorrow evening to firm up plans for Sunday."

"Sounds wonderful. Talk then."

Sally ended the call with a smile on her face and her heart thumping against her ribs. Hearing his voice had set her up to deal with the paperwork littering her desk. A few hours later, she rejoined her team. "Okay, guys, let's call it a week and start afresh on Monday morning bright and early."

The team agreed, and they left the station within minutes of each other. Jack held the passenger door to his car open for Sally; she'd forgotten he was giving her a lift home.

"Do you have anything special planned this weekend?" she asked as he pulled out of the car park and into the sluggish traffic.

"No, nothing really. I was hoping to either put my feet up or get some fishing in. What about you?"

"It's the dreaded boyfriend-meets-the-parents lunch looming on Sunday. I'm a little apprehensive about that."

"You'll be fine. I've met both respective parties, and what's not to love? Is this to do with Simon's suggestion regarding you moving in with him?"

"Yes and no. I'm still not a hundred percent sold on the idea. Maybe I'm just petrified of things going wrong between us like it did with Darryl."

"I think you're being daft. If we all went through life with those kinds of thoughts, no one would ever walk down the aisle or move in with someone else again after experiencing a failed relationship."

"I know. It's easier said than done. Seriously, in my heart, I know Simon is the polar opposite to Darryl, but my head is the one issuing the stark warning."

"It's a tough call. Not one to be taken lightly, I guess." They arrived at Sally's house. "Looks like your dad got your tyres fixed."

"Thank goodness! I'm lost without a car. Thanks for the lift. Want to come in for a quick cuppa?"

"Nah, Donna would serve my gonads up to the kids if I'm late. I rang her earlier and told her what time to expect me. Have a good weekend, Sally. Hope everything goes well on Sunday."

Sally leaned over and pecked him on the cheek. "Thanks, partner. I hope you get some quality 'me time' over the next few days."

She exited the vehicle, waved him off then surveyed her car before she entered the house to a very warm welcome from Dex. "Hello, sweetheart, have you been a good boy?"

His usual high-pitched whine hurt her ears.

"Give me ten minutes to get changed, and we'll go out for an evening stroll." She popped her head around the kitchen door to find her parents talking to each other near the stove. "Hi, thanks for sorting the tyres out, Dad. Let me know how much I owe you."

"We can discuss that later. It was no bother. Any news from SOCO about the car?"

"Damn, I knew there was something I had to chase up this afternoon. Maybe it would have been too soon to learn anything. I'll chase it up on Monday. Do I have time to take Dex out for a quick walk before dinner, Mum?"

"If you want to, love. I can always put your dinner in the microwave. It won't spoil."

"Fab, thanks, Mum. What's on the menu tonight?"

"Chicken casserole."

"Smells delicious, as always. I'll nip up and get changed and shoot off."

"Take care, and don't let Dex off the lead," her father warned as she ran up the stairs two at a time.

After a quick change into her jogging trousers and sweatshirt, they were off. She walked Dex along the usual route down by the river, and he kept pulling on the lead, urging her to release him, but she refused to buckle. Halfway down the track, they came across the same man and dog who had helped her find Dex. "Hello there. I was hoping I'd bump into you again."

"Learnt your lesson about letting him stroll around on his own, I see."

"Yeah, he's eager to be let off, but I can't take the risk now. He means too much to me."

"I better get on. The wife will be wondering where I've got to," he replied abruptly.

"See you soon," Sally shouted after him as he scurried away. "Maybe he was embarrassed about me thanking him again, boy."

Dex looked up at her and panted before pulling on the leash to set off again. They walked another twenty minutes then turned back. Sally strolled past the car on the drive and gasped. "What the fuck? Who would do such a thing?"

She ran into the house and slipped Dex's lead off. "Dad, have you got a minute?"

Her father appeared at the end of the hallway, a frown on his face. "Yes, love. Something wrong?"

She beckoned him, placed a finger to her lips then pulled him outside the front door to show him. Someone had scratched the word *slag* into the driver's door. "What the hell? Did you see anyone?"

"No, they must be watching the house, Dad, waiting for me to go out before they pounce. Did you hear anyone out here?"

"No, we were out the back, eating dinner. You better call it in."

"Christ, what good will that do?" She kicked out at the new tyre then rushed back into the house and up the stairs before the floodgates opened.

Sally's mum knocked on the door a few minutes later, holding a steaming cup of tea. "Your father told me what happened, love. I'm so sorry. Any ideas who could be doing this to you?"

"None at all, Mum. Why would anyone think of calling me a slag? I never sleep around. There's just no call for that type of language."

"Maybe we should invest in some CCTV, keep an eye on the car that way."

"Excellent idea. I'll nip into town in the morning, see what I can find."

"Go with your father. He'll give you some advice and can fit it to the outside of the house over the weekend. Don't hide away up here, love. We're in this thing together."

"I just needed to release my pent-up emotions, Mum. It's been a frustrating week with the case I'm working. This was just the last straw. I'm fine now, looking forward to my dinner."

Her mother bent down and hugged her tightly. "We'll catch the buggers in the act, love. Don't you worry."

Sally stood up and wrapped her arm around her mother's shoulder. "I hope so, Mum. Not sure I can take much more of this."

"Nonsense, you're the bloody strongest woman I know. Shoulders back and move on. Don't let the buggers grind you down, as my old dad used to say."

"You're right. Maybe I should cover the car over with something?"

"If they're going to damage it, sweetie, covering it over won't stop them. Do you want us to get our car out of the garage?"

Cold Case

"No, it doesn't make any sense for the bastards to ruin both cars. Thanks for the offer, though, Mum. I just wish I understood the person's motive for doing this."

CHAPTER FOURTEEN

Saturday flew past too quickly for Sally's liking. That morning, she and her father set off to Norwich to source a decent CCTV camera. In the afternoon, she helped her father fit the camera to the front of the house, tucked alongside the drain pipe, angled at where her car was parked on the drive. She had also called the car body shop her father's friend ran and booked the car in for repair, but they wouldn't be able to get to it until mid-week. There was no way on earth she was going to turn up for work in a car with the word *slag* on the side, so her father had generously offered to run her in every morning. She was sure that Jack wouldn't mind dropping her home each night at the end of their shift.

On Sunday, Sally woke up with the tightest knot in her stomach because of what lay ahead at lunchtime. The whole family had dressed up for the occasion; even Simon turned up wearing a smart grey pin-striped suit. Her heart melted when she opened the door to him and he handed her a mixed bunch of flowers and a bottle of red wine. He also held a box of chocolates, which he presented to Sally's mother when she greeted him warmly. The lunch, and the four hours Simon spent with them, was a complete success. While Sally helped her mum in the kitchen, Simon and her father discussed Simon's renovation idea. Over dinner, they raised a glass for their brand-new partnership.

During their stroll with Dex after lunch, Simon admitted how concerned he was for her safety after he learned of the damage to her car. The way he said it made her feel guilty for delaying her decision to move in with him. However, there were still a few issues that she needed to deal with before giving him her final answer. He was wonderful about it, though, and never once pressured her into making a choice she wasn't ready to make.

Simon left at around four in the afternoon to complete some paperwork he had been avoiding. Once he'd gone, Sally's parents had nothing but praise for her new beau. When her father brought up Simon's offer, his eyes brimmed with tears. Sally prayed that nothing went wrong to sour her parents' view of the man she had fallen in love with.

When Sally took Dex for a short walk in the evening, she shuddered when she had the feeling someone was watching her. She admonished herself and put her uneasiness down to a sudden breeze that had struck up, but even Dex was spooked as the dry leaves swept past them on the pavement.

~ ~ ~

Her father dropped Sally into work at eight thirty on Monday morning. She was surprised to see Joanna already beavering away at her desk. "Morning, Joanna. Why the early start?"

"I left a few things unfinished on Friday, boss, thought I'd come in early to deal with them."

"Anything I should know about?"

"I was delving into whether Drake was in the same prison as Wilson and Jenkinson—remember we were looking for a connection there?"

"I do. And were they?"

"No. So that's put paid to that idea."

"Never mind, we can cross that off our list now."

"Did you have a good weekend, boss?"

"Mixed, really. It started off with my car being vandalised but ended up with my parents meeting Simon for the first time. Thankfully, the temptation to kill each other wasn't on the agenda."

"Vandalised? Didn't someone slash your tyres last week?"

"Yes. Too much of a coincidence, right?"

Joanna nodded. "That's dreadful. Any idea who would do such a thing?"

"I wish I knew. Hopefully, we'll find out soon enough, because Dad and I have rigged up CCTV outside the house."

"What a fantastic idea. Let me know when you have a suspect's image, and it'll be my pleasure running it through the system for you."

"Thanks, Joanna. You're a star."

Jack entered the room just before the end of their conversation. "Have I missed something juicy?"

"More vandalism. Dad had to drop me off this morning. Any chance of a lift home tonight, Jack?"

"Sure. Do you think it's something to do with the case? What about Spike? Could he be behind this?"

"I doubt it's him, but maybe it is to do with the case. Only time will tell, but we've rigged up a camera to catch the bastard in the act, so we should find out soon enough. The car is due to be repaired mid-week, so I might be relying on you for a few days, if that's all right?"

"Of course. No bother, you know that. What sort of damage did they do this time?"

"They scratched the word *slag* into a side panel."

"Slag? You? If it's anyone to do with the case, why would they use that word? *Pig* or *filth*, maybe, but not *slag*."

"All right, Jack, no need to keep repeating it. I hate that word as it is."

"Sorry, boss."

"Apology accepted. You have raised a fair point, though." Sally walked over to the coffee machine. "I'm buying. Who wants one?"

Jack and Joanna both nodded. She returned with their cups and set them on the desk beside Jack.

"I did have something else I wanted to make you aware of, boss."

"Go on, Joanna."

"According to reports, there has been a sighting of Drake in Great Yarmouth of all places."

"That's good news. Was he apprehended?"

Joanna shook her head. "Nope, he gave the officers chasing him the slip."

"We know how that bloody feels," Jack grumbled before taking a sip of his drink.

"Damn. Maybe he has more to hide than we first thought. Another one that should go back to the top of the suspect list. Frustrating, either way. Right, I'll leave you guys to it and go tackle the dreaded post. Give me a shout if anything else comes up. As things stand, we're getting nowhere fast."

Sally retreated to her office for the next few hours. She snuck in a quick call to Simon before starting her daily chores. "Hey, you. How are you this morning?"

"Hey, I'm tickety-boo. How are you?"

"Have you had a poetry lesson overnight?" she asked, laughing.

"Oh, I see. Ha, ha. Sorry. I had a wonderful time yesterday. Thank you again for asking me to join you all."

"It was a pleasure. I'm just relieved that you all got on so well."

"I have to say, so am I. What have you got on the agenda today?"

"Boring paperwork and then more tracking down friends and relatives of the victims. I get the impression this week is going to consist of us chasing our tails a lot. You?"

"Yet another traffic accident to contend with first thing. Not sure if the driver was drunk or on drugs. Amounts to the same conclusion in most cases, bloody idiots. Thankfully, the driver was the only one pronounced dead at the scene. However, the driver and passenger of the other vehicle are fighting for their lives in hospital."

"That's terrible! I hope they pull through. Okay, I better let you get on. I'll ring you this evening."

"At last, something to look forward to at the end of the day. Maybe that will change soon."

Sally noted the hopefulness in his tone. "Goodbye, Simon." She hung up and opened the first of the many brown envelopes littering her desk and sighed.

At around ten thirty, Jack brought her another cup of coffee. "Thanks, matey. I'm gagging for that."

He motioned to the pile of letters in front of her. "I'd offer to help, but I'd just cause you more work."

"Thanks. I appreciate the thought, and fear you might be right."

An enthusiastic Joanna peered around the door. "Some good news finally, boss. Border Control have just rung. They have taken Warren Dean into custody and want to know if we can go down and pick him up from Portsmouth."

Sally punched the air in excitement. "Of course. See if Jordan and Stuart will shoot down there."

~ ~ ~

Sally noted the time on the clock when Jordan and Stuart returned to the incident room—almost five thirty.

"That was quick, boys. I wasn't expecting you to return until about eight. You've brought Dean back with you, right?"

"We left him downstairs with the desk sergeant," Jordan said. "It was an emergency, boss, so we used the siren and lights where possible. He's protesting his innocence. Says he's done nothing wrong to warrant being held by us."

"Does he now? Okay, let's lock him up overnight, shake him up a little, see if that changes his mind. Tell the desk sergeant I'll interview him first thing in the morning."

"Rightio, boss." Stuart left the room to deliver the message and returned ten minutes later just as the team were packing up for the evening.

Jack dropped Sally off at home and got out of the car to inspect her vehicle for himself. He whistled. "Wow, that's a hell of a scratch. Wonder what implement they used?"

"I don't care. I'm just annoyed they tested the damn thing out on my vehicle. Thanks for the lift, Jack. See you tomorrow."

"Want a lift in the morning?"

"Thanks, but I'll get Dad to take me in. Enjoy your evening."

Sally entered the house, which was suspiciously quiet for a change. Even Dex wasn't at the door to greet her. Sally dipped into her handbag and pulled out her pepper spray. *Damn, why didn't I ask Jack in for a cuppa?* She tiptoed up the hallway and into the kitchen. She let out a huge sigh when she found her parents in the kitchen, talking. "Gosh, it was so quiet, I thought something had happened. Where's the boy wonder?"

"He's out in the garden with his chew. You're later than usual, so it's put his timing out. You're interfering with his chew time. Everything all right, love?"

"Yes. I had to wait at the station until one of the main suspects arrived. We've been waiting for him to return to the UK for a week or so. I've told them to throw him in a cell; I'll question him first thing."

Hearing scratching at the back door, Sally crossed the room to let Dex in. His tail mimicked a helicopter's blades, and he leaned heavily against her leg while she stroked him.

"That's excellent news. So you think this man murdered the victim?" her father asked while he laid the table.

"That's what we need to find out, Dad. He's spouting his innocence at the moment. I'll get it out of him in the morning, no doubt."

"Will Jack be there during the interview?" her mother asked, wide-eyed and breathless.

"Don't worry, Mum. Every precaution is taken when we question suspects at the station."

"Glad to hear it. Dinner won't be long if you want to get changed, love."

Sally rushed upstairs and pulled on a clean pair of leggings and sweater as there was a definite chill in the evening air.

After tucking into chicken curry and rice, Sally cleared up swiftly then took Dex out for his evening walk. She hadn't gone far when she had the feeling someone was watching her again. "Come on, boy, let's go home before it gets dark."

She walked home with one eye on the road ahead of her and constantly kept an eye on what was going on behind her. She walked past her car on the drive, and her heart sank as she spotted yet more damage to it. "Jesus, what next?" Scratched into the bonnet was the word *whore*. Sally ran into the house and called her father to assist her. "Dad, we need to view the CD. My car has been vandalised again."

"Bloody hell. In broad daylight. This bugger has got some balls, I'll give him that."

"He won't have soon. I'll rip them off and feed them to the pigs down the road." Sally booted up her laptop and rewound the footage. "There. What the...? I know him."

Her father's gaze darted between Sally and the screen. "Who is it, love?"

"I don't believe it." Tears pricked her eyes, and a lump formed in her throat. "He's the man who helped rescue Dex the other day. Bloody hell, why didn't I realise it sooner? I saw him a few days later, and he couldn't wait to get away from me. I've been sensing that someone has been following me the last couple of nights. I bet it was him."

"Don't beat yourself up, love. We've caught him in the act now. He'll get his comeuppance. Why didn't you tell me that someone had been following you?"

"Because no one was there when I turned around, Dad. It was just a feeling. I didn't want you to think I'd become paranoid."

"Nonsense, as if I'd think that. Right, now we've found out who it is, what are you going to do about it? Do you think he's local?"

"He must be if he walks his dog around here. I'll search through and see if I can get a decent image of him and take it in to work tomorrow, get Joanna to run it through the system."

"That'll only work if he's got a record, right?"

"Yes. If he isn't on the system, then I'll distribute his image around the station, see if anyone can come up with a name."

"At least you have the proof. Sorry about your car, love. People who do this sort of thing must have warped minds; that's all I can say."

"I agree, Dad. At least if I catch him, I can present him with a bill for the damages. I should imagine that's going to be quite hefty, even though Ray is a mate of yours."

"Come on, love, chin up. We deserve a tot of the hard stuff."

Her father left the room just as unexpected tears rolled down Sally's cheek. *Why would this man do this to me? I've never knowingly hurt anyone in my life before. Why me?* Hopefully, his name would show up when she ran it through the system and help put her mind at rest.

CHAPTER FIFTEEN

After her father dropped her off at work, Sally rushed up the stairs to the incident room. She was eager to share the CCTV image with Joanna.

"Morning, boss. Everything all right?" Joanna asked.

"No. My car was vandalised again. The good thing is that I caught the bastard on camera." She handed Joanna the image.

"Bloody hell, that's a great shot of the idiot. Let's hope he crops up on the system. I'll get on it right away."

"Thanks. I'm going to chase up SOCO, see if they have come up with anything yet. I really want to nail this bastard to the wall. It's the man who helped rescue Dex the other day. He must have tied Dex up and then pretended to be a caring passer-by—but why?"

Jack entered the room towards the end of the conversation. "Didn't I tell you it was probably him?"

"Yes, I seem to recall you did say something along those lines. I know... I should have listened to you," Sally admitted through gritted teeth. She hated it when Jack was proved right and she was wrong about a person. "Give me ten minutes, and we'll shoot downstairs to question Dean. The desk sergeant said he had an uncomfortable night in his cell. The interview could go either way. Either he'll be pissed as hell at us, or he'll recognise it's in his best interest to tell us everything he knows."

Jack grunted. "I'm betting the former scenario will be the one greeting us this morning."

Sally walked into her office. Ignoring the post, she pulled out her notebook and began jotting down the questions she intended to ask Warren Dean. Ten minutes later, she left the office again and tapped Jack on the shoulder as she passed. "Come on, let's go get him, Bullet."

The unshaven, scruffy Warren Dean was waiting for them in Interview Room One, a large male PC standing alongside him.

Jack started the recording and recited the relevant wording before the interview began.

"Hello, Mr. Dean. I hope you slept well. I'm DI Sally Parker, and this is my partner, DS Jack Blackman."

His steel-grey eyes held her gaze. "No, I didn't sleep well, but that ain't gonna bother you. Do you mind telling me why I've been forced to leave my truck in Portsmouth and dumped in a cell overnight?"

"Okay, I'll cut to the chase. I've been instructed to reinvestigate a cold case from ten years ago. Your name cropped up as a person of interest in that case."

His eyes narrowed. "What are you bloody on about? What case?"

"The case of Aisha Thomas. Do you remember her?"

"Of course I remember her. She was my neighbour. What about it?"

"We have reason to believe that you and she didn't always get along. Care to enlighten us about your relationship with her?"

"Nothing to tell. Do you get on with all your neighbours?"

"This interview isn't about me. Answer the question," Sally said sternly.

"No, I didn't get on with her. That doesn't mean that I killed the bitch."

"Why the animosity? Why did you set out to make her life hell? Was it just for the sake of it, or did you have an ulterior motive that you'd care to share with us?"

"Ah, I get it. That bloody nosey parker on the other side has put you up to this, ain't he?"

"We have it on good authority from several of your previous neighbours that it would appear you had some kind of grudge against Aisha Thomas. It would be good to hear how this woman managed to get under your skin." Sally had used the word *skin* intentionally to gauge his reaction.

Dean flinched. "So we had a few run-ins, nothing major. We can't get on with everyone in this world."

"But why her? As far as we can tell, she was a very kind, compassionate human being. To be honest, I find it hard to fathom why she wouldn't get on with anyone, especially her neighbours. Was it to do with the colour of her skin, perhaps?"

"Now wait just a minute. You can't go around accusing me of being racist."

"I didn't. Again, one of your neighbours overheard an argument you had with Aisha around the time of her death. They told us that you 'unleashed a torrent of racist abuse'. Why would you feel the need to do that? Please help me understand, Mr. Dean."

"That was a mistake."

"Why? Because you were overheard?"

"No... yes... no. She hit my car, and I was furious. It was a spur-of-the-moment thing, which I regretted the second it happened."

"I'm glad you realised your mistake. Did Mrs. Thomas accept your apology?"

His head dropped. "I didn't offer one. I was embarrassed at getting caught out. I'd had enough by then, couldn't live next door to her anymore and put in a request to my landlord to leave the property and get out of my tenancy agreement. Within a few days, your lot were crawling all over the place, and the woman was dead."

"Did you have anything to do with her death?"

His gaze met hers, and his mouth gaped open for several seconds before he recovered enough to answer. "No. Definitely not. I might have disliked the woman but not enough to want to bloody kill her. I can't believe you're asking me that. Is that why I've been imprisoned the way I have? Because you think I'm the one who killed her?"

"Look at it from our point of view. You showed an open dislike for the woman, and witnesses have told us that you even berated her on a number of occasions. When her death was announced, you fled the scene, moved out of the area. Are you seeing why we should think you're involved in her death? It's not rocket science, Mr. Dean."

He shook his head over and over and clenched his hands tightly together in front of him. "I swear I didn't do it. You're so far off the mark. I heard you lot thought a couple of no-mark petty criminals were to blame. What gives?"

"What gives is that new evidence has come our way to disprove that theory. After re-examining the facts, we now have three—or four—prime suspects on our list. You're right up there near the top."

His upper lip curled. "That's bloody preposterous. How the heck would I get in her house? What DNA evidence do you have that I ever stepped foot over the front doorstep? Nothing—that's what."

He was right. They didn't have a bean of evidence placing him—or anyone else, for that matter—at the scene. "Did you see anyone hanging around on the day of the murder?"

"You expect me to remember that far back? She meant nothing to me. Why should I care what happened to her?"

Sally bashed the table with her fist, making Dean and Jack jump. "Stop giving me a hard time! Drop the frigging attitude and just answer my damn question. Ask yourself this, Mr. Dean: do you really think that being so uncooperative is doing your case any good?"

He held his hands up. "All right, all right, stop tying your knickers in a twist. I was angry with you for hauling my arse in here for doing nothing wrong. Back then, I told the investigating officer that I saw a woman enter the back gate."

"Back gate? To the Thomas house?"

"Yeah. He told me he didn't want to know. Had his suspects all sorted and it was probably one of her friends visiting her, as they were going out that night."

"Why didn't the woman use the front door?" Sally asked, thinking she'd thought the question rather than saying it out loud.

"How the fuck should I know? I ain't a mind reader."

Sally ran an anxious hand over her face. Spike Barker had mentioned a woman with either brunette or red hair. "What colour hair did she have?"

"Ten years ago!" Dean repeated. "How the heck can I remember that? I only saw her for a second or two."

"Try. It's important. Was she blonde?"

He sighed. "Definitely not blonde."

"A brunette? Redhead? Did she have black hair? Dyed purple maybe?"

"You just don't give up, do you? I think it was a light brown, maybe a touch of red in there. Like I say, I can't be sure because it was so long ago."

"Another witness has also highlighted a woman and said that her hair was either brunette or red. That's why I need you to really think about this."

"I just said either brown or red—that's as much as I can give you."

"One last question, and then you can go."

"Are you going to give me a lift back to Portsmouth to pick up my truck?"

"We'll organise that, yes. Why did you leave the property so soon after Aisha's death?"

He shrugged. "I don't know. Maybe deep down, I felt guilty for the way I had treated her. I really can't give you more than that. But that's all I was guilty of. I would never set out to purposefully end someone's life."

"And that concludes this interview, Mr. Dean. Thank you for your honesty. Sorry you had to spend the night in a cell. Maybe if you'd been more cooperative in the first place, all of this could have been avoided."

"Uncooperative? Are you having a laugh? All I did was hop on a ferry and dock in Portsmouth, then your mob picked me up and threw me in a damn cell—and for what? Having a bloody argument with a Muslim girl ten years ago."

"All right, you've made your point. Please accept my apologies. You're free to go."

Sally walked the man back to the reception area and arranged with the desk sergeant to give him a lift back to Portsmouth. She rejoined Jack at the bottom of the stairs. "That's two people who have suggested a woman could be involved in this."

"Can I just say I thought you let Dean off lightly?"

She paused mid-flight and looked at him. "You think? I got the impression he was telling us the truth. He may be a racist shit, but I think that's as far as his hatred goes. I'm prepared to eat my words if I'm wrong. I don't think I am, though."

They continued up the stairs and into the incident room, where Joanna greeted them, her face lit up with excitement.

Sally rushed towards her. "You've got a hit?"

"I think you'll need to sit down first, boss."

Sally dropped into her chair and felt Jack's presence behind her. "Go on."

"The man is Frank Little. He's a petty criminal just come out of prison."

"His name doesn't ring any bells with me. What about you, Jack?"

"Nope, nothing."

Joanna raised her finger, asking for them to be patient. "Here's where it gets interesting: he's just come out of Norwich Prison, and his cellmate was your ex, Darryl."

Sally's hand covered her mouth, and hot tears pricked her eyes. Jack gripped her shoulder tightly before he walked over to the vending machine. Sally was momentarily stuck for words. She swallowed the bile clawing at her throat and whispered one word. "Why?"

Jack handed Sally a cup of coffee and sat on the desk beside her. "This isn't about you, Sal," he said, forgetting her rank and speaking to her as a friend. "This is about him trying to maintain his control over you."

"But why? Does he really hate me that much, Jack?"

He shook his head. "He's sick in the head. We'll make sure the parole board hear about this, and that'll put a nail in his coffin regarding any early release coming his way."

"We need to pick this guy up. I better ring Mum and Dad, make sure they're safe." She tried to stand, but her legs refused to hold her upright, and she flopped back down in her chair.

Jack took control. "There's no rush. Call them on your mobile. I'll get an arrest warrant actioned for Little. Have we got an address for him, Joanna?"

"Yes, I'll organise it if you like."

"Do that. We need to get this clown off the streets and banged up again before he causes any real damage," Jack said.

Sally withdrew her mobile from her pocket. "Dad, it's me. Is everything all right there?"

"Yes, love, the same as always. What's wrong?"

"We've identified the man causing the damage. Looks like he was Darryl's cellmate. I need you to lock all the doors. Don't leave the house until we have him in custody, okay?"

"Dearie me, that is bad news. I'll get on to that straight away, love. Let us know when you pick him up. How could Darryl do this?"

"I have no idea, Dad. Stay safe. I'll be in touch soon." Sally hit the end-call button and took a sip of her coffee. Relief swept through her when she overheard Joanna organising the warrant for Little's arrest.

Joanna hung up and smiled at Sally. "I have some good news to combat the bad you've just received, boss. The warrant for Drake's home address has been issued."

"That's fantastic. Jack and I will go over there right away." Buoyed by the news, she leapt out of her chair—and tipped sideways into Jack. "Work properly, legs," she cursed under her breath.

Jack gripped her shoulders and righted her. "Take it easy. Another ten minutes won't make any difference."

"I can rest in the car." She turned gingerly and walked slowly towards the exit. "Are you coming, Jack?"

He tutted and marched across the floor, a scolding expression pulling at his features. "You are as stubborn as my bloody teenagers at times."

"You say the nicest things to your boss."

"I know. I like to keep you on your toes."

Sally swiped his arm as they walked slowly down the stairs. She held on to the handrail, willing her legs to support her weight at least until she got to the car.

When they arrived at Drake's flat, Sally noticed the curtains twitching in the neighbours' flats on either side. She waved, and the twitching stopped.

Jack rang the bell, but again, there was no reply.

"Do your stuff, ex-soldier man."

Jack inhaled a large breath and shoulder charged the door, which immediately gave way under his burly fourteen-stone frame.

They climbed the stairs and knocked on the door at the top, but it remained closed. Jack shouldered that door open also.

Inside, the flat was an utter mess. Every conceivable surface was cluttered with either newspapers, takeaway cartons, or thick layers of dust.

"Jesus, anyone would think this place hasn't been occupied in months instead of days. Put your gloves on, Jack, more for our benefit than in case we leave any DNA behind." The flat consisted of an open-plan living room-cum-kitchenette, a medium-sized bedroom, and a small shower room. "You search in here and I'll take the bedroom."

"Any idea what we're actually looking for?"

Sally shrugged. "Your guess is as good as mine. Anything kiddie-related or to do with Aisha Thomas. Call me if you're in any doubt."

Sally walked into the bedroom. Her stomach lurched as the smell of stale body odour attacked her nostrils. "How can people live like this?" she muttered under her breath in utter disbelief. After tossing aside everything in the bottom of the wardrobe and finding nothing of relevance, Sally got down on her knees and searched under the bed. Amongst the dead flies and dirty underwear, she saw the edge of what appeared to be a photo album. "Jack... in here."

Her partner joined her in an instant. "This place is bloody insane. I thought living with a couple of teenage daughters was bad enough, but this place is the absolute pits. What have you found?"

Sally flipped open the album and soon wished she hadn't. "Fucking sick! These bastards need castrating."

"For fuck's sake! I agree with you. There's no need to keep punishing yourself, Sal. Don't look at any more." He snatched the album from her hand and threw it on the bed.

"My God, do you think they were pupils at the school?"

Jack shrugged. "I don't know. Why don't we just hand it over to forensics? I couldn't stomach flicking through it to find out."

"Good call. Have you found anything?"

"Nope. I reckon I'm going to go away from here with more than a dozen flea bites, though. I think we should get out of here pronto. Hand it over to SOCO, maybe?"

"I'll place the call. I can't see any links to Aisha anywhere. To me, he's guilty of kiddie fiddling. However, that doesn't mean Aisha wasn't onto him. He might have killed her if he thought she was about to spill the beans."

"Maybe, maybe not. It still doesn't explain the two burglars or the woman seen going into the victim's house," Jack replied.

Sally nodded as she placed the call to alert the SOCO team. They waited for the team to arrive twenty minutes later before they headed back to the station.

"What next?" Jack asked.

Sally contemplated his question for a millisecond. "I'm going to speak to the husband again, tighten the screws there a little, see if he comes up with a name for the woman the witnesses have mentioned."

CHAPTER SIXTEEN

After checking with the desk sergeant to learn if Patrick Thomas was on duty, Sally requested his company in Interview Room One within the next ten minutes.

"That should scare the crap out of him if he's guilty of anything," Jack noted.

They settled down at the desk and drummed their fingers as they waited for Constable Thomas to appear.

The door opened, and a hesitant Thomas poked his head into the room. "You wanted to see me, ma'am?"

Sally intentionally didn't offer a smile. It was time to get serious. "Come in, Constable."

Patrick sat in the chair opposite. "How can I help?"

"Our investigation has lead us to some surprising developments regarding your wife's death, and we need your help clarifying a few points."

"That sounds promising and ominous at the same time, ma'am. Obviously, I'll do what I can to assist you."

"Glad to hear that. I need you to cast your mind back to our last meeting. When I asked you about the money you borrowed from the loan shark, you said a friend lent you the money to repay that loan. Do you mind telling me who that person was?"

He slumped back into his chair, his brow furrowed. "I was asked to keep it quiet, ma'am."

"Any specific reason?"

"The person wished to remain anonymous. I wouldn't want to break that promise, ma'am."

"Not even to save your own skin?"

"Sorry, I'm not with you."

"What if the evidence in this case suddenly pointed in your direction? If your name rocketed to the top of our suspect list, would you divulge the name then, Constable?"

He sat upright again and wrung his hands nervously on the desk in front of him. "If that's the case, then I suppose I wouldn't have an option. Is it the case, ma'am? Am I your number-one suspect?"

"Who was it?" she asked, ignoring his question.

He gulped noisily and looked down at his hands. "If I tell you, is there any way you can keep my name out of it? I'd hate for the person to think I couldn't be trusted in the future."

"You have my word. Who was it, Patrick?" she asked, her voice softening a little.

He covered his face with his hand and whispered, "Caroline."

Sally glanced at Jack, her eyes widening as it dawned on her that Caroline was a redhead. Jack leapt out of his chair and left the room.

Looking worried, Patrick watched Jack exit the room and turned back to Sally. "What? Why are you looking at me like that?"

Sally shook her head. "How naïve could you be, Patrick?"

"I'm not with you, ma'am..."

"Two people during our investigation have referred to a red-headed woman. How well did your partner know your wife?"

"They'd met occasionally at the odd police function, nothing more than that."

"Can you think of any reason why Caroline would visit Aisha on the day of her death?"

"What? No. Is that what happened? She never told me. Why would she visit Aisha and not mention it?"

Sally rolled her eyes up to the ceiling. "I can think of one reason in particular. How well do you actually know your partner, Patrick?"

"No, she wouldn't have... I thought I knew her well. We've always got on together. I admit it was a little strained for a little while."

"Strained? What do you mean?"

He sighed heavily. "No one knew around here. If they'd found out, we would have been forced to work with different partners. Caroline and I used to go out together."

Sally tutted and ran a hand through her hair. "For Christ's sake, and it never crossed your mind to mention this to me at the beginning of this investigation? Are you nuts?"

His eyes watered, and he shook his head. "I don't believe it. Not Caroline."

Jack burst into the room. "I've put her next door."

"Thanks, Jack. Constable Thomas here has just told me something very interesting—he and Caroline used to be lovers."

Jack banged his fist on the table. "What the fuck? You didn't think we should know about that?"

"I'm sorry. I didn't think. I don't believe it... I'm in shock right now. I want to see her."

"No way. I can't allow that. Go back to work. We'll be in touch later today. Not a word to anybody about this, all right?"

The three of them left the room. Jack stood in front of the door to the interview room next door, blocking Patrick's way just in case he had a rash notion to barge into the room and confront his partner.

Once they felt Patrick was far enough away, Sally and Jack entered the room and sat down opposite a startled Caroline. "Hello, Constable Hawk. Thanks for taking the time to see us today. We have a few questions we'd like to ask concerning the cold case we're working on. I'm going to tape this interview. Jack, if you'd like to do the honours?"

Jack started the recording and announced the date, time, and who was present in the room. Sally didn't take her eyes off Caroline, whose gaze was pinned to a point on the wall above Sally's head.

"All right if I call you Caroline?"

The constable nodded but still kept her gaze fixed in position.

"Wonderful! I know how busy you are, so I'd like to get straight to the point. How well did you know Aisha Thomas?"

Caroline's gaze dropped to Sally then swiftly returned to the wall. "I didn't. Met her a few times. Why?"

"Well enough to call at her house for an occasional cuppa, perhaps."

The constable shook her head in defiance. "No, never. Oh wait, yes, Patrick and I called in once when we were in the area. No other time."

"Ah, now this is where we have a problem. You see, one of Aisha's neighbours said they saw you enter the back garden of the Thomas house on the day of the murder. Can you explain why?"

Her gaze dropped to Sally, and her eyes expanded with what appeared to be fear. "Impossible. It couldn't have been me."

"Oh dear, that's not so good. In that case, you wouldn't mind standing in a line-up once we've apprehended the suspect, right?"

"Are you for real? I'm a serving police officer. There's no way I'm standing in a line-up."

"You're refusing to help us with our enquiries? May I ask the reason behind your objection?"

"I've just told you. I'm a serving police officer, and I don't have to do it," she replied through gritted teeth.

"Not even when a superior officer has instructed you to do so?"

"No. Look, your time would be better spent investigating the case properly rather than hounding me to take part in some Mickey Mouse line-up."

"Thanks for the advice. I'll do things my way, if it's all the same to you, as I'm the only inspector in this room."

"Whatever."

"We have the DNA found at the scene anyway that we need to sift through. I'll be needing a sample from you before this interview has ended, if only to exclude you from our enquiries, you understand."

"And if I'm not prepared to give you a sample? They're voluntary, after all."

"Then that would make me delve into your background to see what you're hiding and what you're afraid of showing up. Why are you trying to hinder my investigation, Constable?"

"I'm not. Why don't you leave well enough alone? Patrick has been beside himself since the day he heard his wife's case had been reopened. Why would you put a colleague through all that pain and anguish?"

"Simple. To get to the truth. Anyway, I dispute what you're saying. We've just interviewed Patrick. Here's the thing: he told us something that really sparked our interest."

Caroline glared. "What?"

"Any idea what he might have told us?"

"Haven't got a clue. I'm not into guessing games."

"Why did you do it, Caroline? Jealousy? What was your motivation?"

"Do what? You've lost me."

"Kill Aisha. Was it because Patrick dumped you?"

Caroline's mouth twisted as if she were busy chewing on the inside of her cheek. "You have no idea what you're talking about. What is this? You're pissed off with not being able to find a plausible suspect, so you come banging on my door? This is just too bizarre for words, ma'am," she said angrily, emphasising her final word.

Sally ignored her outburst and pressed on. "So, let me walk through the scenario playing out in my mind. Patrick dumped you, fell in love with Aisha, and they got married quickly. By all accounts, they were head over heels in love, so you thought you'd get rid of her and be there for him during his grief. How am I doing so far?"

"With respect, ma'am, you're talking a load of shit."

"Am I? Okay, I'll continue with the scenario. However, things didn't pan out for you as expected, did they? Patrick was so wrapped up in his grief that he neglected to see how desperate you were for him to confide in you, to see you as something more than just work colleagues again, but that boat had sailed out onto the wide blue yonder, hadn't it?"

Caroline chewed her bottom lip, and her eyes screwed up into tiny slits. "Wrong. Try again."

"Am I? What's it like for the man you fell in love with all those years ago to end a relationship, Caroline? It hurts, doesn't it? Damages the heart, never for it to recover, right? I am right in thinking that you're single now?"

"So what's that got to do with anything? You're talking shite."

"I don't think so. You had the ideal opportunity. Patrick had volunteered to work extra hours that evening, and you knew the likelihood of him coming home early was zilch. Therefore, it was the ideal opportunity to make your move. How am I doing?"

"Ever thought of being an author, ma'am? That's a pretty vivid imagination you have. It would be a shame to waste such a talent."

"And that's a pretty sarcastic tongue you have in your head, Constable." Sally heaped on the pressure, hoping to see a chink in Caroline's obstinate façade. "I'm intrigued. Did the conversation ever arise between you?"

"What conversation?"

"About you and Patrick getting back together again. You sharing his bed once more, now that his wife was no longer an obstacle?"

She shook her head and laughed. "Are you sure you should be an inspector, ma'am? Because you're saying things a shrink would say."

"And when was the last time you visited your psychiatrist, Caroline? Recently?"

The constable's glare intensified. "That's none of your goddamn business."

"So, you admit to seeing one then. May I ask why?"

"No. It's personal."

"Was it hard dealing with the rejection? Working alongside him every day, not being able to touch him, to whisper sweet nothings, unable to hug him when he needed a hug?"

Tears welled up in Caroline's eyes. "He was even more out of reach when she died."

"Sorry, can you repeat that louder for the recording? Are you saying that you were hoping to rekindle the love you once had with Patrick?"

She threw herself back in the chair and placed her hands on her head. "Yes. We were soulmates until the day he met her, then everything changed between us. She wasn't good enough for him. She hounded him for a child he didn't want, even took out that damn loan without his knowledge. What sort of devotion is that from a wife?"

"So you killed her?"

"Yes! All right? Yes, I killed her. I couldn't take it anymore. Listening to him complain about how he couldn't perform in bed and that she had been driven to seek out fertility treatment because of his inability to father a child in the normal way."

"Really? She said that? He told you that? Or was it all up here?" Sally prodded her temple with her finger.

Caroline fell silent for a moment.

"Where did Wilson and Jenkinson enter the equation? You are the one who ended their lives, too, yes?"

"Bloody idiots. They were a nuisance to society. Patrick and I had picked them up a few times, slapped their wrists, and always sent them on their way. It didn't prevent them from robbing someone else's home in the neighbourhood. I put paid to their shenanigans because no one else was prepared to bang them up. The opportunity arose to point the investigating officer in their direction, and I jumped on it."

"How did they end up dead?"

A huge smirk developed on her face. "That was easy. I made out I was a bent copper, dangled a lucrative job under their nose. They hopped in my car, and I drove them out to the forest to a supposed meeting with a top man. The gullible idiots took my word for it, and I finished them off."

"You thought you had got away with three perfect murders, but the thing is, you screwed up, Caroline. If you'd only killed Aisha and gone on your way, this case would never have been reopened. Once Wilson and Jenkinson's bodies were discovered, it blew the case wide open."

"Not sure how."

"You're forgetting one minor detail—the bite mark on Aisha's arm. It didn't match either burglar." Sally aimed an imaginary gun at the constable and pulled the trigger. "Pow! Game over."

Suddenly, the door burst open and Patrick stormed into the room, heading straight for Caroline. Jack tipped his chair in his haste to prevent Patrick from getting to Caroline, but it was too late.

"No, Patrick!" Sally shouted when she saw something glinting in his hand.

Jack tussled with Patrick, grabbing his arm when he broke free. But by that time, Caroline was lying on the floor, blood spouting from the wound in her neck where the knife was embedded. "Why? You crazy fucking bitch, why did you have to kill her?"

Tears trickled from Caroline's eyes. She lifted her head two inches off the ground, and the movement took her breath away. "Because I loved you," she managed to say before the light faded from her eyes.

EPILOGUE

Over the coming few days, Sally and her team tied up all the loose ends to what had been a heartbreaking and frustrating case.

A search of Caroline's flat had uncovered several pieces of Aisha's jewellery and numerous pictures of Patrick pinned to a notice board beside her bed. Poor Patrick didn't have a clue. Sally felt sorry for the man who had lost the love of his life through someone else's obsession with him, but that didn't excuse the fact that he had punished his partner by killing her before she had been brought to justice. Sally promised to put in a good word for him with the Crown Prosecution Service. She was prepared to plead with them to go with a lesser charge.

Another force had finally arrested the paedophile Drake, who was on remand, awaiting a court appearance after admitting that he had touched up several pupils at Highfield School. He'd warned the kids that if they spoke out against him, terrible things would happen to their family members. The children were receiving counselling at the school.

The man guilty of vandalising her car and torturing Dex, Frank Little, was picked up the day after the warrant was served, and he was also awaiting trial at the remand centre.

After sitting down with their colleagues for a celebratory drink, Jack dropped Sally home on Friday night. He and Donna were heading off for the weekend without any kids in tow. Sally had her own exciting weekend to look forward to—she was about to meet Simon's parents.

Sunday lunch came and went without a hitch, and Simon insisted on dropping her home. He pulled the car to a stop at the end of her road and switched off the engine.

"Okay, what's going on?" Sally asked, tilting her head.

He turned in his seat to face her. "Well, now we've both met our respective parents, where do we go from here?"

"I thought you were driving me home," Sally said, feigning confusion.

"Sally Parker, you would bloody drive a nun into prostitution."

"Really? Not sure how you work that one out." She sighed heavily. "All right, yes."

"Yes?"

Sally leant forward and kissed his open mouth. "Yes, I'll move in with you... on one proviso."

"Name it."

"We have joint custody of Dex. We have him at the weekend. How's that?"

"Of course, it goes without saying."

"Right, take me home. You can break the news to Mum and Dad."

His mouth dropped open again.

"I'm kidding, you bloody idiot. They'll be delighted for us, I promise."

He kissed her, pulled away, and held her face between his hands. "I promise you only good times from this day forward. I will never disrespect you or mistreat you. I give you my word on that."

"I know. I love you, Simon Bracknall, for being the type of man every woman is desperate to have in her life."

"I love you, too, Sally Parker, just for being you."

THE END

NOTE TO THE READER

Dear Reader,

What a heart-wrenching read that was.

The question is; did Sally and her team enjoy tackling a cold case enough to investigate more of them in the future?

There are some tough decisions on every front to challenge Sally in the next book.

Yet another case that will touch your heart, I guarantee it.

Get your copy today.

http://melcomley.blogspot.co.uk/p/deadly-encounter.html

Thank you for your support as always.
M A Comley

Reviews are a fantastic way of reaching out and showing an author how much you appreciate their work – so leave one today if you will.

Printed in Great Britain
by Amazon